Bumbled LOVE

LILA ROSE

USA TODAY BESTSELLING AUTHOR

D1557154

Bumbled Love Copyright © 2021 by Lila Rose

Editor: Hot Tree Editing
Photographer: Wander Book Club
Cover Designer: Covers by Juan
Interior Designer: RMJ Editing & Manuscript Service

Bumbled Love is a work of fiction. All names, characters, events, and places found in this book are either from the author's imagination or used fictitiously. Any similarity to persons live or dead, actual events, locations, or organizations is entirely coincidental and not intended by the author.

First Edition
ISBN: 978-0-6487998-7-0

CHAPTER ONE

BROOKE

*R*eagan and I had been best friends for a long time. We considered each other family, and I would honestly be lost without her. I was a little miffed that she was gaining the attention of Carter Anthony, quarterback to the Wolves, because it meant I would be seeing less of her. However, my happiness for her outshone anything else.

I wished I had something like what Carter and Reagan had. Not that they were together yet, the chase was still happening, but I could see the lovey-dovey gazes they shot each other. Even if they were oblivious to the other's attention.

It was sweet, soft, and so cute.

Something I wanted to find.

Then I'd met Dustin Grant. He was at the bar with Carter,

because they were friends and teammates, and I'd thought there was a connection between Dustin and me when we'd made eye contact... or it could have been just me being a sex-depraved hussy since Dustin was Fine with a capital F. But he was sweet, funny, and charming. Also, he hadn't seemed fazed by the talk of sex toys, and I'd thought he could make me smile and be giddy like Carter made Reagan.

So, days later, when I saw him down the street one night and we started talking, I'd let my mind consider that something could spark between us. It didn't matter he wasn't my usual type, since I loved men in suits and who had the smarts to take on the world, but there was something about Dustin and his carefree, cute attitude that appealed to me. Hence, when I'd asked him what he was doing the next night, I hoped he'd get the hint and ask me out. He'd told me he was in a bind, that he had some lunch event he had to attend with a date but wasn't sure he could go because he had other commitments.

Of course, I played it cool and said I could help out. He had smiled, which had my nipples perking up from their deep sleep when he told me my help would be fantastic. After our discussion, I'd floated away in a daze without gathering more information besides how to get to his house and each other's phone numbers.

The next morning, full of those butterfly feelings about the date with Dustin, I rang my nana on the way to let her know.

"What?" she answered.

"Good morning to you too, Nana Bev."

"Yeah, yeah, it's too early to be chirpy."

It was early, but Dustin had said it was a lunch charity event that was an hour away. "But I have good news."

"Please, pray Jesus, tell me you're knocked up and I'm finally gettin' a great-grandbaby?"

"Well, no—"

"Then I'm goin'."

"Nana Bev, this could lead to having a baby." Okay, I was thinking way ahead of myself, but the thrill of knowing I was going on a date made me say it.

"All right, I'm listenin'."

"I've got a date."

"Boy or girl?"

My nana knew I was bisexual, and it didn't faze her as long as I was loved and she got a great-grandbaby out of it before she died. Those were her words exactly.

"A guy."

"All righty. Now tell me you've tidied up your probably-grown-over bush since you haven't seen any action in a damn long time."

"Jesus, Nana. You don't need to worry about that."

"Fine, fine. But do you need advice on how to find your G-spot—"

"I'm hanging up now, Nana."

She cackled like the crazy lady she was. "Love you, boo, and good luck."

"Love you too, and thanks."

Taking one last look in the rearview mirror at my subtle but classy makeup, I then checked my new short black dress and heels. Everything was still in order, so I climbed out of the car and headed for Dustin's apartment.

After I knocked, the door opened quickly, and I smiled warmly at the sight of Dustin in his fancy suit. A sigh slipped past my lips as my gaze traveled over him.

"Hey." He grinned. "Thanks so much for doing this. Come on in." His words confused me a little, so when he walked off, I quickly stepped in and shut the door before following him down the hall and into the living room.

Then froze.

"Benjie, this is Brooke." Dustin curled his hand over a boy's shoulder, who was Dustin's mirror image.

"Brooke, this is Benjie, my six-year-old son."

Son.

His son.

A boy from his loins.

"Benjie, Brooke's here to look after you."

I was there for Benjie?

My stomach twisted at my own stupidity. Seriously, where had I gone wrong in that conversation on the street?

Still in my state of shock, I slowly turned when I heard footsteps approaching.

"Hi, baby. I'm a little early, but I thought since it's far away, you never know how traffic will be." A gorgeous woman eyed Dustin over my shoulder as she swayed her hips our way. Her gaze snapped to me and ran over my body before a smirk lifted her lips. She strode by me and curled herself around Dustin. "Who's this?"

"Letta, this is Brooke. She's taking care of Benjie for me."

An urge to punch Dustin in the balls, or myself in the tit for reading the conversation wrong, hit me. What stood in front of me was nothing like I thought would happen.

The woman ran her eyes over me again and giggled. I wanted to rip her tits off at the patronizing sound. Like she *really* knew I had read the situation wrong. But how could she?

You're wearing heels and a slutty little black dress, idiot.

The only thing I could do was pretend that I didn't make a fool of myself by thinking Dustin wanted to go on a date with me.

Forcing a smile, which I hoped wasn't scary, I said, "Benjie, it's cool to meet you. I don't usually dress like this for fun, but I had to pop into work early for a meeting before I could have the day off and didn't get a chance to change."

Benjie shrugged and gripped his dad's pants. He looked unsure, which I didn't blame him for, since I was a stranger to the poor boy. Did Dustin have strange women mind his son often? If yes, it was bad form. Anyone could be a crazy lady.

"Hey, how about we go for a drive for some ice cream, and we can stop at my place so I can get changed? We could even go to a park." I pulled my gaze up to Dustin and ignored the tart near rubbing herself over him in front of his son. "If that's okay with you?"

"There's a booster seat in the garage you can take. But what do you think, buddy?" He smiled down at Benjie.

Benjie shrugged. "I'm okay with it."

Dustin chuckled, and I wanted to throat punch him, disgruntled it sounded nice and deep. "I'm sure you're okay with ice cream and the park."

Really, could I blame Dustin for the whole mix-up? I wanted to—boy, did I want to—but it wasn't completely his fault. I'd been dazzled by his looks and charm.

Dammit. It would have been easy to blame Dustin wholly.

Benjie's lips twitched. "Maybe?"

Hopefully, I could make this day better—even when my skin itched with a flush of embarrassment—by spending time with a six-year-old kid and having fun. I would make the best of my day off.

What could also help my mood was punching Dustin in the balls. Then again, Dustin and I would have probably been terrible together. Really, this saved me from a crap date.

"Great. Let's hit the road, kid, so we can get the fun started." I held my hand out and hoped Benjie trusted me enough to take it. He looked up to his dad one last time, who smiled and nodded, before he walked across the floor and took my hand.

His was so tiny in mine.

A pang of want hit me in the chest.

For a while now I'd been thinking about having a family to call my own. While I had Nana Bev and Reagan, even her family, I wanted children. I wanted a man or woman who I had a connection with and could call my own.

"Thanks, Brooke. You two have fun and we won't be late."

Turning, I waved over my shoulder. "No problem." If I hadn't been petty, I would have told him to have fun, but I wouldn't have meant it and Nana always said lying was a sin.

By the time I got Benjie in his booster seat, Dustin and his date were already outside ready to take off. Ignoring them, I climbed into the driver seat and looked over my shoulder to Benjie. He was frowning while looking out the window at his dad.

Starting the car, I asked him, "What's your favorite ice cream, Benjie?"

"My real, real favorite?"

Smiling, I nodded. "Yep."

"Chocolate."

"Hmm, I do like that, but mine's caramel from the store where you can add mix-ins."

His eyes widened. "Like candy?"

"Exactly. What to try it?"

"Yeah! My friend told me all about it, but I haven't tried it yet."

"Today's your lucky day then. We'll get one of those and go to a park close to my house. I've heard it's pretty good, but you can be the judge of it."

He gave me a big toothy grin. "Okay."

By the time we reached the park, ice cream covered Benjie, but he'd managed to finish it. Of course I'd eaten mine back at the shop, since I didn't know kids took forever and a day to eat them. The mess didn't bother me, since I didn't have the best of cars and I'd also changed into tracksuit pants and an old tee. All things could be cleaned. My mood had lifted a lot, happy to see Benjie smiling as he talked about his LEGO and the things he liked to build with them.

"Okay, a few rules before we play."

He looked up at me and nodded, holding my hand tighter.

"First, we make sure we can see each other at all times."

"Got it."

"Second, we don't talk to strangers."

"My dad tells me that one."

"Good." I smiled. "Lastly, we have fun."

He giggled. "Let's go." He wiggled my arm up and down before I dropped it and took off running, glancing back to see he followed and was laughing louder.

We went on the swings, slides, across the fort a million times, and even played in the sandpit. I hadn't had so much fun in a long time. Benjie was such a cute little kid.

"Hey."

Turning from Benjie on the swing again, I smiled at a man who seemed in his forties. "Hi."

"You look like you've had fun. Not many mothers get out there and play with their kids."

"Oh, he's not mine. I'm minding him for someone."

He nodded, and I didn't miss the way his gaze dragged slowly over my body. Even in my old clothes, a flash of heat lit his eyes. I found it slightly sleazy at a park when there were kids around. I mean, maybe people picked up in parks, but I knew I wasn't going to be one of them.

"I have a daughter. She—"

"Stranger danger. Stranger danger," Benjie shouted as he came running up and pointing to the man beside me.

Laughing, I took Benjie's hand and told him, "Benjie, it's okay."

His brows pinched together. "But you don't know him, right?"

I couldn't lie. "No, I don't."

His eyes widened. "Then he might take you to his car and kill you. You have to be careful, Miss Brooke."

Miss Brooke. I loved it when he first said it at the ice cream parlor, and I loved it now.

Biting my bottom lip to stop my smile, I nodded down at

him. "This is true." I looked to the man. "Sorry, the plan was to not talk to strangers. I have to stick to it."

The guy snorted out a laugh. "How about I get your number—"

"No!" Benjie yelled and started pulling me away from him. Grinning, I threw up a hand to the guy, as if to say, "What can I do," and followed after Benjie.

Besides, I was happier spending time with Benjie than talking to douches who hit on women at parks.

After some more time playing, Benjie and I walked back to the car. I shook Benjie's hand in mine. "Hey?"

"Yeah?"

"You hungry?"

"I could eat."

This kid. All day he'd made me smile. "How about we get some takeout on the way back to your place, since it's getting late?" We'd eaten lunch at the food truck not far from the park but had gone back since I promised Benjie some more time on the slides.

"Can we get chicken nuggets?"

"Chicken nuggets are a must."

"Yay!" he cried, jumping into the car.

This kid had so much energy, I wished I could steal some. By the time we got back to his house and had eaten, though, he was finding it hard to keep his eyes open on the show we were watching in the living room.

"Do you need a bath or shower before bed?"

"Nah, I'm not stinky." He quickly looked away, which made me think he was supposed to wash before bed.

"How about I start the shower for you, get it to the right

temperature, and you have a quick wash before hopping into your pajamas."

His lips thinned as he thought it over. "No thanks."

Ruffling his hair, I laughed. This kid was awesome. "Okay, what do you want to trade for a shower?"

"Huh?"

"You can ask for something, but as long as you have a shower for whatever it is you want."

"Really?"

"Yep." I nodded.

"Okay, let me think." He tapped his chin a few times. "I'll wash if you come back another day to play?"

Damn.

Well, I couldn't really say no to those bright eyes, and I was sure Dustin would need help another time for one of his other dates. I ignored the dip to the belly over that thought and reminded myself Dustin and I wouldn't be good together anyway. "Fine, *but* I'm just not sure when it'll be." I held out my hand. "Deal?"

He took it and shook. "Deal."

After he showered and dressed in Spider-Man pajamas, Benjie yawned and looked over at me on the couch. "Can you read me a story?"

"Of course. Want to do it while you rest in bed?"

He nodded, and together we made our way down the hall to his bedroom, which was decked out with everything a boy could think of. There were more superheroes, LEGO, and Transformers than I'd ever seen in one room.

Benjie hopped into bed and pulled the covers up. He held a soft bunny toy under one arm and looked up at me. I helped tuck him in before moving over to the shelf that held books. "What are you in the mood for?"

"Anything."

"All right." I picked one out and moved over to sit beside him on the bed. My heart warmed when he curled into me and rested his little head on the side of my arm. "Ready?"

"Yep," he said, popping the *p*.

It didn't take long for his eyes to close as I read about a wizard called Harry Potter, which I was sure I'd seen a movie of. Even after he'd fallen asleep and started drooling on my arm, I stayed there reading because I wanted to enjoy myself with this little monster.

"Hey," I heard, and I let out a little yip as I looked to the doorway.

Dustin stood there with a smile on his face. For a moment I'd forgotten where I was and whose child I'd been taking care of. I quickly adjusted Benjie to lie down and stood from the bed, leaving the book on the bedside table. I snuck on my tippy-toes to the door and pushed Dustin out of the way.

"He's asleep." Why I had told him the obvious, I didn't know.

Dustin chuckled. "I can see that. Sorry I got back so late."

Waving it off, I walked back down the hall and into the living room. "It's fine. Benjie's a heap of fun to hang out with. I may have promised to do it another day to get him in the shower."

Another chuckle from Dustin sounded, and I still wanted to throat punch him for the way it caressed over my skin.

Why did I like the sound of his voice?

"Anyway, I better go. See you around." I grabbed my bag

and started for the door. Along the way, I happened to notice the woman he took wasn't around.

Unless she's in his bedroom waiting for him.

Shut up, brain.

"I really appreciate this." Dustin stopped at the door when I stepped out.

I nodded, then when I couldn't think of anything else to say, and since I didn't want to look at him any longer because he still looked good, I made my way down to the car.

I headed to my cold, quiet home and wallowed about having no one there to fill the rooms.

God, I was pathetic.

But at least I had found a new friend in Benjie.

CHAPTER TWO

DUSTIN

Carter couldn't keep the smile from his face, and I couldn't blame him. Somehow, he'd magically gotten invited to move in with the woman he'd been pining over for a while. They'd known each other back in high school, and he'd always had a crush on her. It was damn cute how smitten he was. I'd only met her once and could already see good things for them. She had no idea he was into her, so it'd be fun for North, another friend and teammate, and I to see how Carter worked his magic, since this was a rare scene. Usually he was a tag-and-bag-them type when it came to women.

Shit, as I thought about it, maybe I was the same as Carter. It was easy for me to get a woman. Any woman.

Was it time for me to settle down and find someone like Carter was?

Hell no. I'd already done that when I was younger—and I got something special from it, Benjie—but I wasn't ready to be tied down again.

"Your face is going to break if you keep smiling like that."

Carter glanced at me, chuckling. "I wouldn't care." He pulled over to a sweet little house. "This is it."

"You sure this is what you want?"

"Yes. Are you sure you want to waste your Saturday helping me move in instead of doing something better?"

Carter had helped me out a lot, same as North. I'd do anything for those two. "Yeah, I'm good."

"Shit." Carter's eyes widened at something over my shoulder. I turned in the seat and saw two older men shoving at each other as they made their way toward the car.

Carter had mentioned Reagan's dad was a fan. "That her dad?"

"Yes, and the other is Tom. He works with Reagan as the principal."

Clapping, I rubbed my hands together. "Let's get this show on the road." I opened the door as they arrived and climbed out. I was sure I heard a couple of gasps.

"Mr. Wild, it's good to see you," Carter said as he walked around the car.

Mr. Wild didn't look at Carter but stared at me as he replied. "Herb, son. Call me Herb."

"And call me Tom."

They looked away from me to glare at one another.

Carter cleared his throat. "Herb, Tom, I'm sure you know this is—"

"Dustin Grant."

Did they just *sigh* my name?

"Hey, great to meet you both." I held my hand out and Tom nearly got there first until Herb slapped his hand down and took hold of my hand first. He gave it a rough up-and-down shake.

Tom punched Herb in the arm. "Not so hard, you'll hurt him."

I glanced to Carter as Herb dropped my hand and Tom gently shook it before stepping back. Carter hid his grin, and I expected laughed behind his fist.

This was crazy and yet entertaining at the same time.

The women soon arrived. Reagan quickly skipped down the path. "Hi, Dustin, did you come to help?"

Wasn't it obvious? I didn't say the words, since I could see how nervous she was already with the quick, frantic glances she sent Carter. "Sure did, but I didn't realize you'd have so much help already. Hey, Brooke," I added to the woman who, over a week ago, had helped me out by minding Benjie, who wouldn't stop talking about how much fun he had with her.

A blush hit her cheeks and she wouldn't meet my gaze, but she asked, "How's Benjie?"

A smile lifted my lips. "He's good. With his momma this weekend."

Brooke nodded and said no more.

Strange. What had also been weird was how she practically ran from my apartment when I got home after the work event. I'd enjoyed seeing Brooke reading to Benjie, even though he'd been sound asleep. I'd thought we could have a chat, get to know one another better since our two friends were, no doubt, going to be dating eventually. But she backed out of there like her panties were on fire.

Hmm, what type would she wear?

Fuck, that thought was a little too creepy.

Reagan broke the silence by getting Herb and Tom moving to unpack the truck. "Dustin, this is my mom, Elaine. Mom, Dustin. Also a football player."

Stepping forward, I took hold of Elaine's hand she had outstretched and brought it to my lips for a quick kiss. "Lovely to meet you, Elaine." Christ, I had to tone back my charming side, but I'd done it out of respect, like I would anyone older than I was.

Elaine giggled. "You too, Dustin."

"Elaine," Herb barked. "Come here." I didn't miss the glare he shot me. I fought my grin as Elaine actually curtseyed and scurried off to Herb, who scowled at me some more.

Carter chuckled. "Guess I'm still his favorite."

Herb ran a finger across his throat as he stared me down. I bit back my own laugh.

"Dad," Reagan yelled. "Stop threatening him."

Herb huffed and quickly grabbed a box to follow Tom and Elaine into the house. I could already tell I was going to have some fun around these people.

"Dustin, whatever you see or hear today, please don't be scared. My family is a little—"

"Crazy," Brooke quickly supplied with a grin. "It's why I love them." Then to my surprise, she swatted Reagan on the ass and went to the back of the vehicle for her own box to carry in.

Grinning at Reagan, I shrugged. "All good, babe. As long

as that's a thing in the family, slapping butts, I could get used to— Fuck." I coughed out a breath after Carter elbowed me in the side. Yeah, there was no way in hell I would be going anywhere near Reagan's ass. Not that I was going to in the first place; still, it was fun to tease. "I'll keep my hands to myself." I shook my head and mock scowled at Carter as I went by to get another box before I made my way into the house. It was a homey place, not too big, but it'd be perfect for Carter and Reagan to get to know each other better.

When I heard voices down the hall, I walked that way and found a group in there unpacking some things. I dropped my boxes to the bed and ripped one open.

Snorting, I picked out a pair of Carter's boxers. "I don't know how Carter can wear these. Though, he told me once he doesn't like his testes being restricted, which is why he's a boxer guy. I prefer a tighter type of boxer...." Everyone stared at me like I'd grown another head. "Just in case anyone was wondering."

Herb huffed. "We weren't." Guess I'd still have to work on getting back into his good graces. Which meant I'd have to tone down my charm. It'd be hard, since I was always charming, even if I said so myself.

A noise caught my attention from the doorway. "Jesus Christ, Dustin." He lunged for his boxers and snapped them out of my hand before shoving them back in the box and closing it. "Is nothing sacred with you?"

"What? We're all guys here—"

"Hey!" came a voice from the corner. Brooke.

Shit, I hadn't really taken notice of who was in the room.

Wincing, I offered, "Oops, sorry, forgot you were in the room."

Brooke's jaw clenched, and I knew I'd screwed up before she threw the box she'd been unpacking to the floor and walked out. She'd forgive me, right? I mean, I was the forgivable type.

Reagan glared as she hit me in the back of the head. Rubbing it, I cried, "What was that for?" I hadn't said anything that bad.

Reagan shook her head at me, spun around, and followed after Brooke.

Tom snorted. "You two don't know what you've got yourself into hanging with them."

"What did I do?" I asked the room. All right, I knew what I'd done, but I hoped for a little comradery from the men in the house at least.

Herb looked to Carter. "Is he always that stupid?"

Carter nodded. "Yep."

"How am I stupid?" I asked. They acted like I'd done the worst thing in the world.

Tom sighed. "If you weren't on the Wolves, I'd hit you myself."

Throwing my hands up in the air, I asked, "Why?" I didn't get the big deal. Yes, I'd forgotten Brooke was in the room, which surprised me since she was a stunner, but it wasn't the end of the world.

Was I missing something they saw, and I didn't?

Herb went to say something until Tom placed a hand on his arm and shook his head. Herb nodded. "You're right. He needs to learn on his own."

Learn what, dammit?

"And if he doesn't, we kick his ass. Just not too much. He'll have to play still."

Well, at least they still liked me somewhat. Though, what they'd need to kick my ass over, I wasn't sure.

Since I wasn't getting answers from these bastards, I made my way to the door. Carter asked, "Where are you going?"

"Obviously, I need to figure out what I did. I'm going to ask the women." Because it couldn't have only been about me not seeing Brooke in the room. There had to be something else. I heard laughter behind me but ignored it. Though, when I heard voices in the kitchen, I paused, just as Carter caught up to me. "What are you doing?" he whispered.

"They're talking." And it sounded interesting.

"So?"

I pressed a finger to my mouth. "Listen."

Herb and Tom arrived and leaned in with us as Elaine said, "The only advice I can give you both, without knowing fully what's going on, is that men can screw up a lot. Sometimes it's good to just forgive their stupidity. Other times it's better to make them pay while they grovel for forgiveness."

Brooke's reply was quick. "Another thing to do would be to go out tonight, get tanked, and sleep with a random to get over everything."

Tensing, I stepped back. The conversation kept going and the others stayed listening, but I moved down the hall a little as my gut tightened.

Whatever I did had made Brooke want to go out, get drunk, and sleep with someone.

LILA ROSE

Why did the thought of that threaten to have my breakfast come back up?

Slipping into the bathroom, I shut the door after me and leaned against it. It wasn't an easy feat, trying to figure women out and the way their minds worked.

What could I have done to have pissed Brooke off to make her want to drink and... that other thing she said? My jaw clenched, and I fisted my hands as abrupt anger hit me.

Shaking my head, I pushed the emotion aside and tried to put the puzzle pieces together, because I didn't like the thought of upsetting Brooke so much it would drive her to *that*.

Brooke had been happy when we spoke down the street before she came to my place to look after Benjie. Even at the house she seemed okay. She'd said she had just come from work.... Wait a damn moment. She hadn't come from work. Unless she had the day off, but then why would she say she came from work when she'd been dressed in that hot black—

Fuck me, I'm a dumbass.

The conversation ran through my mind. I hadn't said I needed help minding Benjie. Brooke could have taken the whole thing as me needing a date to the event.

I hit myself in the forehead.

She'd dressed up for me.

She'd come to the house to go on a date with me, and I'd thrown Benjie at her. Then, fucking *then*, Letta walked in, and now I felt like the biggest moron in the world.

Brooke must have thought me the biggest asshole ever. I could have kicked myself. Shit, I even wanted to punch myself right then and there as my gut twisted.

If I was honest with myself, and if I could go back in time, I would have taken Brooke over Letta in a heartbeat. Letta was a leech. I hadn't seen that in her the first time we'd met, but she showed her colors when she kept talking about how much I made playing football. I would have had fun with Brooke. I knew it from the night at the bar. She'd seemed easygoing, smart, and a little fiery.

Although, if I had taken her, Benjie wouldn't have had such a good day. He'd hated all babysitters I'd gotten for him in the past. Brooke was different. They'd hit it off.

Shit.

What did I do now?

Sighing, I scrubbed a hand over my face. I didn't have a clue what to do. I wasn't ready for anything long-term, and I had a feeling Brooke was a long-term kind of woman.

I couldn't deny she was attractive. She was. Her curves were made to be grabbed and held, and caressed, and loved upon.

But all I could offer was friendship. Especially now Benjie had connected with her.

Right, it had to be friendship. I had to put what I'd figured out in the back of my mind and go out there acting like the blind idiot I'd been so they didn't figure out I knew I'd fucked up.

Still, friendship was good. She'd eventually forgive me for being a dick, and we'd become friends.

Yeah. Friends were what we were supposed to be.

Right?

So then why did the thought of Brooke going out and hooking up make me want to throw up?

Groaning, I slapped my forehead once again. I just had to walk out there and go with the flow. See what happened.

All right. Easy.

Stalking to the door, I opened it. "Whoa, I wouldn't go in there for a while."

You dickhead. Why didn't you think of something else to say? Now they all thought I was in there crapping myself and stinking out the toilet.

Thankfully, students from the school Reagan worked at showed up and took the spotlight away from me. In the end they stayed and helped us unpack the truck before we rested for lunch and had a quick game of catch. Throughout it, I tried to talk with Brooke to settle into the start of our friendship, but she ignored me and moved away.

I was man enough to admit it hurt. Though, I couldn't blame her.

As I tossed the ball to a kid, I asked Carter, "What do you think of Brooke?"

Carter caught the ball next and threw it back to one of the kids. "She's nice. Funny."

Nodding, I watched as the kid grabbed it out of the air. "Yeah."

"Dust, don't fuck around with her."

Did he know something?

"I won't. I think I hurt her feelings earlier." My not noticing her wouldn't have helped the situation I'd already dug myself in.

Carter stared at me like he was amazed at my stupidity. "You think?"

All right, I didn't think it, I knew it. "Yep. She hasn't

spoken to me since. She's good with Benjie." I threw the ball back. But knowing she was good with Benjie wasn't all I could think about. Even though I'd fucked up that day, she had gone with it and had taken on Benjie for me so he wouldn't think she wasn't there for him. Although, I would have done the same, embarrassed about the situation.

Seriously, I could still hit myself for it.

Reagan cried out one of the kids' names, and I realized my throw had hit him in the nose and blood gushed.

Fuck.

At least he hadn't seemed fazed by the hit, and after a little while, lunch still went ahead. We all sat at the outside table together, and my gaze kept drifting toward Brooke as she smiled and laughed with the others.

Yeah, I didn't want her to go out drinking and hooking up because of something I'd done. But how could I stop it?

It wasn't until we neared the end of the day, I had an idea. Tom had offered to give me a lift home, but as we got outside, I approached Brooke. "Hey, you mind dropping me home?"

She tensed. "I thought Tom was going to."

"It's out of his way. You're sort of heading in that direction."

Sighing, she asked, "How do you know I am?"

"I figured since we saw each other in that area, you were over my way."

When Brooke winced, I regretted mentioning the day we saw each other on the street.

"Sorry, I can't. I have things to do."

Was that code for she had men to do?

"You can't put it off? Benjie would love to see you."

Her brow rose. "Isn't he at his mother's?"

Shit.

"Right." I had to think of something else. "Look, I didn't want to say anything, but I'm kind of scared of Tom knowing where I live."

Her lips twitched when she looked away from me.

"Dustin, are you ready?" Tom called. He had a glint to his eyes, and I widened mine at Brooke while I held a finger up to Tom.

A soft laugh fell from her lips, but then she shook her head. "I can't take the fun away from Tom, sorry. Besides, I work for the man, and if I take this away from him, he'll make my life hell."

I had a feeling she was right. Dammit.

Sighing, I scrubbed a hand at the back of my neck and nodded while I thought of something else to stop her going out tonight. If I asked her not to, it would make her suspicious.

"Good luck, Dustin. Tell Benjie I said hi." Brooke turned and started for her car.

My gut gripped and I wanted to call out to her, but I couldn't think of anything to say. I'd dug myself into this one, and I would have to deal with it.

For now.

Until we became good friends.

Then I could tell her not to go out and sleep with random people.

Right?

CHAPTER THREE

BROOKE

$\mathcal{T}$apping my pen to the notepad, I stared at Ariel and waited for her to tell me why she made an appointment with me. I waited some more as she looked around the room and drummed her fingers on the armrests of the seat.

Being the school counselor had its advantages of helping the students. It also had its disadvantages of time wasters just trying to get out of a class.

"Ariel, are you going to tell me what you needed to see me for?" When I first asked why she made the appointment, she'd said she needed to talk to me. Only she wasn't talking to me.

She shrugged and bit at her thumbnail. "Things."

"Great, that's a start. What things?"

"Bell said you helped her with talking to her parents about

her being knocked up. That's really cool of you. I reckon if you hadn't, they would have kicked her out."

"I'm not sure they would have. Is that why you're here? Are you pregnant, Ariel?"

"Eww, no. I'm not stupid."

Frowning, I told her, "Ariel, are you calling your friend stupid for being pregnant? That's not nice. Bell will need support not only from her family but her friends as well."

She paled a little. "Shit, that *was* mean. I didn't mean it. Bell's not stupid. Accidents happen. At least she and Troy love each other."

"Watch your language, please."

"Shit—crap—ah, hell. Sorry, Miss Baker."

Rubbing a hand over my mouth to hide my smile, I nodded. "That's okay. But are you able to get to the point on why you wanted to see me?"

"Sure."

She said nothing else and once again looked around the room.

"Ariel. None of your teachers have come to me, so I know you're not struggling in class. Has something happened at home or within your friend group?"

"Nope, that's all cool."

Some days I wanted to wring their little necks when they were like this. Sighing, I dropped my notepad and pen to the desk and leaned back in the chair. If she wasn't here to tell me something, maybe she wanted to ask for information. "Ariel. Is there something you want to know?"

Her eyes brightened. "Yes. You know how Miss Wild and

Carter Anthony are living together, are they like *together,* together or just friends?"

Dear God. Didn't the students have enough to deal with instead of wanting to hear all the gossip from their teachers' lives?

"Ariel, is this really why you made an appointment to see me? To ask about a teacher's life?"

Her cheeks pinked. "Well, you're Miss Wild's bestest friend. I thought you would have the inside scoop."

"And you thought I would actually tell you?"

She bit her bottom lip and nodded. "Yeah."

"I'm sorry, Ariel, you thought wrong. There will never be a time I speak to students about a teacher's life. Now, is there anything else you needed?"

Her head dropped back as she groaned before she leaned forward and begged, "Please, Miss Baker. Please tell me."

"No, Ariel."

She rolled her eyes. "Fine. So, can I get some condoms?"

"Ariel—"

"They're not for me. Well, in a way they are, but it's just so others think I'm cool that I'm having sex." I stared her down, and she added, "Okay, I might use one if something happens at the party this weekend."

I pray for the students of today.

"Having condoms isn't something cool. They're there to provide people who are sexually active protection from sexually transmitted infections and becoming pregnant. Being sexually active isn't cool either. It isn't something to brag about. It's meant to be a special moment in your life to share with someone you trust immensely."

Ariel snorted. "Yeah, right. Do you know how many horny boys there are out there? They'd say and do anything to get into our panties."

I believed it because it happened even in my time. Hell, it was still happening.

Sighing, I slid open my drawer and took out the basket of condoms. Ariel stood as I placed it on my desk in front of her. "Just because you have some condoms, don't run off to the next boy who shows you interest. Find someone who is willing to wait, who loves you for you and not what's between your legs." She giggled. "And make sure you're on birth control *and* he uses a condom."

"Sure," she drew out.

Doomed. All the kids were doomed.

Shaking my head, I waved her off. She skipped out of the room quickly, shutting the door behind her. Leaning back again, it was my turn to groan. There was a 50 percent chance my students listened to me. Those who did, I hoped I helped where I could, and it was for the better. Those who didn't... well, there wasn't much else I could do besides tying them up or offering the girls a chastity belt because they were just as horny as the guys.

Honestly, it blew my mind the number of students I knew of who were sexually active. I lost my virginity at nineteen and that was with a boyfriend I'd been with for three months. Why couldn't they all be like that instead of dating a guy for a couple of days and giving it up to them?

A knock sounded on the door. "Come in."

Tom stuck his head in with pinched brows. "A boy has his penis stuck in a glory hole in the senior bathroom."

Scooting my chair back, I waved my hands in front of me. "What do you want me to do? I'm not going in there."

"Brooke—"

"Tom. I'm a woman. He's a male student. You've got to deal with this one. I'll be on the girls when they get their periods or anything else, but I am not talking to a boy right now when his dick is stuck. If he needs advice after it, I'll help."

"Fucking hell." He scrubbed a hand over his face and stepped into the room. "Do you have anything I can cut the plaster with?"

"He'll scream the halls down if you come at him with something sharp. Is he, ah, still hard?"

"Yes! Because he keeps trying to pull out so it's rubbing.... I am not finishing that."

Our lips twitched.

"Okay, tell him to stay still while he thinks of gross things and let it go down. He'll be free soon enough. Please tell me you have the toilets closed off." If someone caught him in that predicament, it would be hell.

Tom rolled his eyes. "Of course. I am the principal; I do know things."

"And yet you came to me for advice. Who found him? Please don't tell me it was another student? If it was, we need to get them to keep their mouths shut."

"It was another teacher, thank God. I better get back there."

"Good luck," I called as he walked out and heard him muttering under his breath.

Tom, and even Reagan's parents, always made me miss my own. It had been a tragic day when I lost them in a car accident when I was thirteen and Nana Bev took me in. I still missed them and made sure to remember all of our time together.

Still, I didn't go without; Nana made sure of it. She might be harsh and rough around the edges, but she was amazing. She hadn't had to take me in when I had aunts in other areas of the world who were willing. But I heard she'd threatened that if they tried to take me, she would hurt them in ways they wouldn't be able to walk for the rest of their lives.

Many were scared of her. Others thought she was crazy. I just loved her for who she was.

She'd been disappointed when I told her about the mistake I'd made with Dustin. Only she ended the conversation with "Chin up, sweet pea. There's other cock in the sea."

I'd snorted and replied with "You mean fish, Nana."

"Fish, cock, whatever floats your boat. You know I don't care."

I did.

My phone chimed, and I looked at the clock. I had time to peek at the text before my next student showed. Picking it up, I saw the name and thinned my lips. I met Rebecca the night after I helped Carter move in with Reagan. I'd gone to the bar, and she'd caught my attention. We'd talked, shared a little kiss, and exchanged numbers, but nothing other than that because I hadn't wanted to go further, since my head had been muddled with thoughts of Dustin, even when she was willing.

Rebecca: **Hope your day is better than mine.**

It was attached with a picture of what looked like dog shit everywhere. Rebecca was a veterinarian.

Me: **Okay, yours looks shittier than mine so far.**

Rebecca: **Ha, I thought it would. How about a drink tonight to help cheer me up?**

My phone chimed again, and another message popped up. One that had my belly fluttering.

Closing my eyes, I shook my head and cursed my gut. Where were the butterflies when Rebecca's name popped up?

Why did they have to act up when I saw *his* name?

Dustin: **Hey, Brooke, sorry to put you on the spot, but is there any chance you could look after Benjie tonight?**

Goddamn.

Benjie or Rebecca?

Me: **Sorry, but I've got other plans.**

Rebecca: **Damn. Hopefully another time.**

Me: **Definitely.**

Sighing, I opened Dustin's message again and paused over it. I wasn't doing this for Dustin.

I wasn't.

This was for Benjie since I promised I would come back.

Me: **What time?**

Dustin: **Six, if that's okay?**

Me: **I'll be there.**

For Benjie.

Dustin: **Great, see you then. Thank you!**

I didn't bother replying. Instead, I placed my phone in the drawer and shut it.

My stomach gave off another flutter.

Cut that shit out.

The man didn't like me. I was doing this for Benjie. Dustin would be there for five minutes, so surely I couldn't go back to crushing on him in that time. Actually, I refused to let myself be swayed by his big smile and muscles and humor.

He hadn't wanted me.

He preferred his women slim, tall like him, and absolutely gorgeous. I wasn't putting myself down. I knew I was okay-looking or else people wouldn't approach me. But I wasn't slim, and I wasn't tall either.

Not that I cared what he liked.

I didn't.

We were acquaintances for his son's sake. Really, it would be simple. I would show, ignore his charm and looks, and spend my time with Benjie. Easy.

THIS TIME I WORE JEANS AND A SWEATER SINCE THE WIND HAD picked up during the day. I knocked on the door and waited. Those damn butterflies were back. I heard a pattering of foot-steps, and the door opened to a smiling Benjie.

"Miss Brooke," he cried before throwing his arms around my legs.

Grinning, I rubbed a hand over his head of blond locks. "Hey, Benjie. It's good to see you."

Dustin appeared in the doorway, giving me a smile just like Benjie's. "He's been excited for your arrival."

Laughing, I glanced down at the boy still hugging me. "I can see that."

"Benjie, how about we let Brooke in?" Dustin shifted back with a hand to the door.

Benjie took my hand and dragged me in. "Come on, come

on. I have some Play-Doh we can play with, or there's always LEGO. But I got a new coloring book with superheroes in it. We can share."

"Everything sounds great."

He pulled me into the living room, and I couldn't help but look around for that woman who had been there the other day, but it seemed no one else was around.

"Look!" Benjie pointed to the coffee table in front of the big television. He had all his things set out.

"I can't wait," I told him honestly. Seeing Benjie happy made me happy. He went over to the coffee table and got to his knees. "What do you want to start with?" I sat beside him.

"Hmm." His eyes danced all over the table. "I don't know."

Laughing, I ruffled his hair. "What about the coloring before we get messy with the Play-Doh?"

"Yes!"

"Sorry to interrupt."

Jolting, I looked over my shoulder. I'd forgotten Dustin was still there, and from the smirk on his lips, he knew it as well. "I have pizza coming soon, but I need to duck out for a moment."

"Bye, Daddy." Benjie didn't even look at his dad. He was too busy pulling his pencils toward him and lining up all the colors between us.

Glancing back to Dustin, I nodded. "Okay, take your time. We've got lots of things to do."

We shared a smile, and my heart tugged. I quickly looked away.

"You can do this page and I'll do this one," Benjie instructed.

"Deal."

"I'm going now."

"Bye again, Daddy."

"Later." I waved over my shoulder before picking up the red pencil for Spider-Man's costume.

"Will I be missed at all?" Dustin asked.

"Nope," Benjie and I said together and started chuckling. Benjie got to his little feet and ran around the couch to hug Dustin, who returned it.

It was nice seeing the soft look on Dustin's face as he stared down at his son. My heart tugged again. Fucking organ. One day I would have my own family, but it wouldn't be this one.

I drew my attention back to the coloring and heard Dustin leave before Benjie joined me on the floor again. I bumped his shoulder. "How's school?"

He shrugged. "It's boring."

"It'll get better. Do you have friends?"

He smiled. "Yeah, heaps."

"That's good."

We went on with our own pictures with the television on in the background. It wasn't until we'd started on the Play-Doh that there was a knock on the front door.

"I'll get it." Benjie went to pop up, but I took his arm.

"How about you finish the kitty and I'll get it?"

"Okay." He dropped back down quickly. We'd been making farm animals with lots of laughing and talking. I'd questioned having a cat on the farm, but Benjie informed me quickly that there had to be one for it to chase the mice. Still,

Benjie's favorite was the cow. Though honestly, it looked like a penis with legs. Not that I would tell him that.

Expecting it to be the pizza, I grabbed my purse and headed for the door, casting another gaze around the spacious area. Dustin certainly had a nice house. It was just the right size for both of them. Opening the door, I smiled, only it dropped away when I saw a woman on the other side and no pizzas in sight.

"Can I help you?" I gripped the door so she didn't push her way in. No doubt Dustin being a football player, he'd have some stalkers around.

"Is Dustin home?" A small smile was on her lips. It seemed my glare didn't affect her.

"No, he's—"

"Mommy!" Benjie rushed down the hall, skidding to a stop before launching his small body at his... mom.

Shit.

"I'm sorry," I offered quickly. "I didn't know who you were. I'm just here watching Benjie while Dustin ducked out for a little while. He should be back soon and then I'll be going—"

"Miss Brooke, no, you can't go. We haven't played LEGO yet."

Benjie's mom, Dustin's ex-wife or girlfriend—I wasn't sure if they'd married—giggled at her son when he wiggled out of her arms and wrapped his arms around my legs again.

"It's all right. Stay as long as you want. I'm just here to drop this rabbit off." She opened her purse and pulled out a stuffed bunny.

"Bugs," Benjie yelled and gripped the rabbit to his chest.

"Remember when I asked if you had everything before you left for Daddy's?"

"Yes," he said sheepishly.

"Next time you double-check everything. I knew you wouldn't be able to sleep without him."

Benjie nodded as he averted his eyes away guiltily.

She looked at me, and her hand came out. "I'm Emily. You must be the Miss Brooke I've heard so much about."

Smiling, I took her hand and shook it. "Just Brooke. It's nice to meet you." Stepping back, I gestured inside. "Please, come in."

"Yes, Mommy. Come in so I can show you what Miss Brooke and I have been doing."

Her eyes lifted to mine. "You don't mind?"

"Heck no."

"Okay, but only for a little bit." She slipped by me, and all I could wonder was why Dustin and she broke up in the first place. She was beautiful with her long black hair and dark green eyes. It was obvious Benjie loved her wholly. Where in the hell did it go wrong? Then again, maybe I didn't want to know, because I hated to think of my chances for a future if these two couldn't make it.

Following them down the hall, I found it a little awkward I was in Dustin's house with his ex and the mother to Benjie. I hoped I didn't say or do anything stupid for her to think she didn't want me around her child.

CHAPTER FOUR

DUSTIN

*H*ey," I called to the pizza delivery guy. "I'll grab them." I took the steps two at a time to the front porch of my house. I handed over the money for the pizzas, and the kid shrugged, gave me the boxes, and took the money —which I'd forgotten to leave in the first place. Luckily, I hadn't really needed to go anywhere. It'd been a ruse to get Brooke over here so our friendship could start. I planned for Benjie to warm her up before I got back, and she'd stay to have pizza with us while we got to know one another.

It would be better for Reagan and Carter if we were friends. That was what I kept reminding myself when she rocked up in a simple sweater and jeans, which seemed to hug—

No, I wasn't going there.

Unlocking the front door, I slipped in and made my way down the hall when I heard giggling. At the mouth of the hall to the living room, I stopped. I hadn't even seen my ex's car out front; I'd been too keen to get inside. Yet, there she was, sitting on the floor with what looked like Play-Doh eyebrows.

"Pizza," I called.

Emily's gaze lifted, and she smiled. I was lucky to have a good relationship with her after our breakup. Benjie jumped up from the middle of the women and ran at me with Play-Doh sideburns, but I noticed Brooke had turned to face me with a Play-Doh mustache.

Smiling, I braced as Benjie knocked into me with a hug. "Looks like you guys are having fun."

"We are." Benjie nodded, his gaze on the pizza boxes. The women got busy removing their facial hair and putting them in the containers.

Tapping Benjie's nose, I told him, "Go help pack up the Play-Doh and then wash up before we eat."

With a quick nod, he raced back over to the coffee table and helped while I ducked into the kitchen to put the pizzas down. When I got back into the living room, Emily stood and brushed off her pants. "I better get going. Benjie, give Momma a kiss, and I'll see you in a couple of days."

Benjie did, along with a tight hug.

Brooke quickly bounced up. "I'll walk out with you and leave these two to dinner."

It didn't slip by me that she kept looking away from me.

"No, Miss Brooke. You have to stay for dinner. Please, please, please stay so you can read me a book later."

Good job, Benjie. I wanted to chuckle and rub my hands together like an evil villain would. My plan was working.

Emily smiled down at our son and met my gaze. She nodded, to what I wasn't sure. She looked back to Brooke. "You can't say no to that, right?"

I hadn't expected help from my ex. Though, I was grateful for it.

Brooke nibbled on her plump bottom lip, and my cock gave a jerk in my jeans in response. Her eyes flicked to me and back down to Benjie. "I'm not sure—"

"There's plenty of pizza," I added.

Her brows dipped. I could tell she wanted to run, but as she looked back down to Benjie, who had his hands clasped in front of him silently begging, her expression softened.

"Okay. I'll stay for pizza, but then I'll have to see what the time is. I'll need to get some rest for work tomorrow."

"What do you do?" Emily asked.

"I'm a high school counselor. It can be challenging sometimes."

Emily snorted. "I bet."

"What about you?" she asked, like they were starting a new friendship and bonding.

Why hadn't she ever asked me questions?

"I'm in real estate."

Before they could continue this little chummy chat, I butted in. "Em, didn't you have to get going?"

"Oops, you're right. Dustin, walk me out."

"Sure."

"It was lovely to meet you, Brooke."

"You also, Emily."

Emily bent and kissed Benjie on the cheek, and with another tight hug, she started for the door, and I followed. When she stepped outside, she turned back. "Benjie adores her, Dustin."

"You're not worry—"

She waved me off. "No. I think it's great. She's a sweetheart with him. I really like her."

"Good. She enjoys spending time with Benjie, and I trust her with him if I need to go to some event or something. Saves me leaning on you all the time when it's not even your turn to have him."

"You know I don't care, and I agree, she is trustworthy. Is there anything between you two?"

A lot of exes didn't get along, but Emily and I got together when we were young, and I think that was what burnt us out. We'd loved each other, but in the end the love was more for a friend than a partner or lover. She would always be in my life, and I couldn't help but be thankful, because she was a great woman. We were open with each other, which was how I knew she'd started seeing someone, but Benjie hadn't met him yet.

Shaking my head, I admitted, "She's a good friend with Carter's woman—"

"Carter has a woman?" She gaped.

Chuckling, I leaned against the doorsill. "Well, not yet, but he's a goner for her. I'm trying to get on Brooke's good side and become friends since we'll be in their lives no doubt."

Emily crossed her arms over her chest. "What did you do?"

"I— What?"

"Brooke seems pretty easygoing. What do you mean you're

trying to get on her good side? Was there a bad side to begin with?"

Sighing, I scrubbed a hand over my face. "There was a small misunderstanding."

"Dustin."

Quickly, I rambled, "She thought I had asked her out, but I already had a date set and I'd intended her to mind Benjie. I didn't realize until a few days later."

Emily winced.

"Exactly my reaction when I figured it out."

Emily reached out and patted my arm. "Good luck."

"Thanks."

"And there's nothing else you want besides friendship with her?"

No. Yes. Maybe were the first words in my head.

"Friendship right now."

"Well, you better get in there and work your charm. Just don't overdo it and act like a douche."

Scoffing, I spread my arms wide. "When do I act like a douche?"

Her brows rose before she started laughing and walking off.

"Real nice, Em."

"Bye." She waved over her shoulder.

Grumbling under my breath about not being a douche, I made my way back down the hall and into the living room. Only no one was about. I walked into the kitchen and found them sitting at the counter with plates of pizza in front of them.

"Was there something you liked?" I went over and flipped

a box open, drawing my own plate close to pile it with some meat lovers. When Brooke didn't answer, I looked at her. Brooke's gaze roamed over me with heat to her cheeks.

Interesting.

Did that mean she liked what she saw?

Fuck it, of course she did. I knew I was appealing to the opposite sex. I couldn't help but flex a little as I drew some pizza up to my mouth. Not that I was supposed to flex; friends didn't do that for each other.

"Miss Brooke liked the Hawaiian one like me." Benjie beamed at Brooke, who smiled back, redder than before.

"Good to know." I winked at Benjie. "How come Momma was here?" I'd forgotten to ask Emily.

Benjie glanced away. "I forgot Bugs."

Leaning over the counter, I tapped his nose. "Make sure you double-check everything. Saves Momma coming this way, yeah?"

"I will," he said a little solemnly and took a small bite of his slice. I noticed he'd managed two pieces already.

"Good, kiddo. Though, at least it was good Brooke and Momma got to meet this time."

Benjie brightened. "It is good." He turned to Brooke. "Now you can come to my other house too, and we can play there."

Brooke laughed as she reached out and hugged Benjie to her side. "I'll have to see, buddy." My son was an awesome kid; it was good to see Brooke had already noticed it. Her fondness for him was obvious.

What about me?

I was talking about friendship fondness though. Benjie started talking about a book he wanted to read since he'd heard it was good from a friend, and as I ate, I watched and listened to them. It was like she'd been around him more than a couple of times. Like they'd known each other longer. Benjie usually took a while to warm up to people, yet he hadn't with Brooke. That said a lot about her.

Yeah, I wanted to get to know Brooke as well.

"How was work today?" I asked when the conversation broke away.

She glanced at me and then down to her pizza. "Good. Though, I had a student make an appointment to see me because she wanted to question me about Reagan and Carter."

"Can I go play for a little bit?" Benjie asked.

"Go for it," I told him with a wink.

I caught her tense when he bolted from the kitchen, but she picked up her slice and took a bite. "How long do you think it'll take Carter and Reagan to get together?"

Her smile was soft. "Not long. Anyone with eyes can see they're half in love already. Besides Reagan."

"They're good for each other."

She nodded. "They are." She wiped her hands on some paper towel she or Benjie must have gotten out. "You weren't gone long before."

Grunting, I shrugged. "I thought it would have been longer. Do your family and Reagan's get along?"

Her gaze shifted behind me to the doorway. Was she thinking of running?

"My parents passed away a long time ago. I have some aunts and uncles elsewhere in the world, but it's been Nana Bev and me for a while."

"Sorry to hear about your parents. I don't see much of mine since they're in Texas."

"So, you are a cowboy?" She smirked.

"Born and raised."

"Where's the accent gone?"

"It comes and goes, darlin'."

Her lips parted when I put on the Texas tone. Since I'd lived out of the state for a damn long time, I'd lost a lot of it. It only showed when I drank.

Brooke cleared her throat. "Right. That's, ah, cool." She stood and picked up Benjie's plate along with hers, moving over to the sink. I quickly stuffed the rest of my pizza in my mouth and walked around the counter, stopping at her side as she rinsed the plates. Her hand swept out for my plate. I gave it to her and rested my hip against the counter.

"Benjie loves hanging out with you."

There was another soft smile for my son. When was I going to get one?

"He's a great kid."

"Sorry about Emily showing. I didn't expect you'd meet my ex that soon."

Her brows shot down. "But you expected us to meet?"

"Well, yeah. Unless you're going to stop seeing Benjie."

"No, I wouldn't do that to him."

"Good."

She put the last plate in the dishwasher and faced me. "Emily seems really nice."

Smiling, I nodded. "Yeah, everyone loves her. People were shocked we split up, but we got together young and drifted in different directions. The only thing keeping us together had been Benjie. Before it soured, we wanted to end it while we were still friends."

Surprise was written on her face, in her eyes, brows, and mouth. "That's... really amazing. There's not many couples who do that."

Shrugging, I smiled. "Yeah, I know. But it was the best for Benjie as well. This way we spend all the major holidays together. Christmas, Thanksgiving, and Easter as well. When I'm not playing, that is."

"Do you get annoyed with work dragging you away?"

She was asking me questions. Wanting to know me. This was damn good.

"Sometimes it pisses me off, but then I get on the field, and I'm lost in the game. It's still a thrill. Do you like what you do?"

A laugh dropped from her plump lips.

Lips I had to stop looking at.

Jesus, what the hell was wrong with me? I was trying for friendship and yet everything she did had my attention. The way she shifted, when she brushed her hair behind her ear, her lips, eyes, body... fuck me.

Friends, jackass. I had to remember my mantra.

"I have my days. Today wasn't one of them. What is it with boys and their junk?"

Sputtering out a chuckle, I asked, "What?"

"It's like you can't keep it in your pants. A teacher found a boy in the restroom with his dick in a handmade glory hole in the wall. He'd gotten stuck."

That time I roared my laughter. "Oh shit, that poor kid."

"Poor kid? Poor Tom. He'd come to me for advice. I told

him the kid will need it to go down before being free. Tom went back and told this kid, and do you know what he did?"

"Ah shit, he didn't?"

"I suggested to Tom to tell him to think of gross thoughts, but no, apparently this kid decided to finish so his dick went down before he escaped."

"What did Tom do?"

"Ran from the room when the kid wouldn't listen and waited for him to finish. The kid didn't even care he'd done that around teachers."

"Couldn't Tom get in trouble if the kid says something?"

She snorted. "Who will he tell? He was scared a fellow student would find out, but he didn't care about the teachers. Tom also filed a full incident report, called his father, and told him what was happening while the kid, ah, finished."

"Jesus, I would never show my face again."

"We'll see if he comes—" I chuckled at her choice of words. Her cheeks pinked and she groaned. "Wrong choice of word there, but you know what I mean."

"At least not all boys are like that," I offered. "I had a friend who would have done the same if he'd thought of it. His sex drive was crazy. He'd jack off in the bathroom all the time. Me, I'd prefer to do it in the privacy of my bedroom."

Brooke straightened. "I should get going."

What did I say?

It was then I noticed before she cruised by me that the pink on her cheeks had deepened, and her eyes had heated.

Sweet Jesus, she was picturing me handling myself.

Why did that please me so much it sent a bolt of desire to my cock?

"Benjie, I've got to get going, sorry," I heard before I followed her with a damn huge smile on my face. She caught it when I stopped beside her and glared.

"But, Miss Brooke, what about reading?"

"I'm sure your daddy would love to do it, and I promise next time I'll stay to read."

His hand shot up with his pinkie out. "Pinkie swear?"

Brooke grinned and hooked her pinkie around his. "Pinkie swear." She bent to hug him, and I wondered if I could ask for one.

It was too soon probably.

"I'll walk you to the door."

Brooke picked up her bag and shook her head. "No, it's fine. Thanks, ah, for the dinner and... yeah. Bye." She swiftly went down the hall and then I heard the front door open and close.

Poor Brooke seemed flustered. I'd have to remember to bring up masturbating again around her.

CHAPTER FIVE

BROOKE

A few days later I still couldn't keep the thought of Dustin jerking off from my mind. Even as I watched Tom eating a banana at lunch, it popped into my mind.

"You're creeping me out." Tom glared.

Rolling my eyes, I muttered, "Whatever."

"I went over to Carter's parents' house for dinner," Reagan announced.

Tom dropped his banana and gripped his head. "Please tell me you didn't do anything stupid."

Regan sighed. "You have no faith in me—"

"Do I need to remind you, and you, for that matter," he pointed at me, "that there have been multiple occasions where you two got into some type of trouble for saying something stupid or falling over your own feet or burning something down?"

"One time I burned a part of my kitchen. One time," I said.

"I'll admit I'm clumsy sometimes, but you have nothing to worry about. Dinner went well." Reagan's gaze moved to me. "Carter's brothers were there."

I knew where this was going. "Is that right?"

"Yes. Casper and Calvin. You remember them from the game we went to?"

"I remember you being blind to the fact they were his brothers and father sitting there."

She scowled. "Shut up. I could ask Carter if they're—"

"No."

"But—"

"No."

She sighed. "Fine. I also met Carter's sister and her husband, who's in a biker club."

My ears perked up.

"A biker club, you say?"

She grinned. "I do—"

"No," Tom grunted.

"But—"

"No." He glared. "Don't even think about it." He stood and pointed at his eyes with two fingers, then at us. "I'm watching you two. Brooke, I love you like another dysfunctional daughter, but you're not dating a biker. Reagan, don't even think about a biker."

"I'm not. Carter already said no to State when he mentioned partying at the clubhouse."

"Knew I liked that boy." His gaze narrowed again and

49

landed on me. "Find a nice woman or man to settle down with or you're going to give me a heart attack."

Lifting my hand, I shot him a salute. "I'll see what I can do, Captain."

He sighed, shook his head, and walked out of the lunchroom.

Glancing back to Reagan, I leaned in. "So," I drew out. "When can I meet Carter's sister to get an invite to the biker club?"

She gulped and paled a little. "We're having both families over for dinner next week. They'll be there and you have to come as well."

Grinning, I rubbed my hands together. "I wouldn't miss it." I knew, just knew, it would be a wild ride having the Wilds, Reagan's family, and Carter's together.

"You can help me keep Dad in check."

Snorting, I picked up my coffee. "We're talking about Herb here. He'll do and say whatever comes to mind."

She shuddered. "That's what I'm worried about."

It might have been mean to be looking forward to something at my best friend's expense, but I was excited to see what would happen.

THAT WEEKEND, I DIDN'T EXPECT TO HEAR FROM DUSTIN ABOUT minding Benjie since, from Reagan, I knew the guy's team was at an away game. So as I sat on the couch in a hoodie and pajama shorts watching *The Handmaid's Tale*, my phone buzzed. Presuming it would be Reagan, surprise flittered through me when Dustin's name flashed on the screen. A sudden bolt of concern hit me in the chest. Was Benjie okay?

Dustin: **Hey Brooke. Can I ask a huge favor for tomorrow if you're not busy?**

Sighing, I relaxed back on the couch.

Me: **What's up?**

Dustin: **Emily was called in to work to show a few houses. Are you able to watch Benjie for a while? She would have texted you herself but didn't have your number.**

There were no set plans for me tomorrow, and I did want to see that latest Disney movie. It'd be good to have a child with me to watch it. At least then the strange looks wouldn't happen like they would if I went on my own. Not that I cared too much.

Me: **Sure. I'll need the address and it would be good to grab Emily's phone number. Plus, would either of you mind if I take Benjie to that new Disney movie?**

Dustin: **I'm sure he'd love it and Em would be fine with you taking him. You're the best, Brooke. I'll talk to you when I get home.**

He left me the address and phone number for Emily, who I texted asking what time I was needed. No other family would I do this for in my only spare time, but since I had a bond with Benjie, he was the lucky kid who was never going to get rid of me.

With my plans set, I watched a few more episodes before going to bed, while looking forward to seeing Benjie.

I rocked up the next morning just a little before ten to a cute one-story house. Before I was even out of the car, the front door opened with a bang, and Benjie was running down the walkway screaming my name.

Smiling wildly, I braced for when he wrapped his arms around my legs. Only that time, I couldn't resist. I had missed the little booger, it being five days since I'd last seen him. Bending, I picked him up and hugged him close so he curled his tiny arms around my neck.

Benjie pulled back. With his hands on my shoulders, he gave me a shake, which had me laughing. "Mommy said you'd be here and said you're taking me to the movies. I can't wait!"

"Me neither."

"Thank you again, Brooke." Emily approached with her arms full of things. "Usually I have a couple of people I can rely on, but they're all busy." Her eyes widened. "You didn't have any plans already and Dustin talked you into this, right?"

Shaking my head, I smiled. "No plans." Great, now I sounded like a lonely loser. I hadn't even told Reagan about seeing Benjie again. I didn't want it to seem like I was using the kid to see Dustin, because it wasn't that at all. Though, I knew my girl wouldn't judge me.

I placed Benjie back on his feet and took the booster seat.

"Here's your bag, Benjie."

"Thanks, Mommy."

She leaned down to kiss his cheek. "Be good for Miss Brooke."

"I will."

Emily straightened. "There's a spare key in Benjie's bag if you get back before I do."

"Okay, thanks." I was simply happy she trusted me with her son.

The movie was amazing, and by the way Benjie was throwing his arms around as he spoke about it, he loved it also. We stopped at the front of the movie theater while I waited for him to finish talking before we decided to either go and eat or play in the arcade that was next door.

"Brooke?"

Turning, I saw Rebecca approaching me.

Benjie trailed off from talking and took my hand when I waved to Rebecca. "Hi. Did you just see something or are you going into one now?"

She smiled and briefly glanced down to Benjie before training her eyes back on me, ignoring the boy at my side. It rubbed me the wrong way.

"I'm going into one in a moment with a friend. What about you?"

"Benjie and I just saw the new Disney one." Looking down, I grinned at Benjie and swung our hands at our sides. He beamed up at me.

He looked to Rebecca. "It was awesome. There was—"

"That's nice." Rebecca smirked at him before looking back at me. My imaginary hackles rose. I knew I mentioned I didn't have any kids when we'd met at the bar, but it didn't mean she could brush off a child I was spending time with. "I was going to call you this afternoon. I'm hoping you'll go out on a date one night this week?"

After seeing the way she acted around Benjie, there was no way I would want to see her again.

"Sorry, I can't. I'll be busy with Benjie."

Her nose screwed up. "You said you didn't have any kids."

"I don't. He's my friend." I grinned down at Benjie who returned it.

"You're picking him over going on a date with me?"

"Yes."

Her gaze narrowed. "I thought you were different."

Snorting, I shook my head. "I thought the same about you." Turning to Benjie, I asked, "What do you want to do next? Lunch or the arcade?"

"Arcade!"

Laughing, I ruffled his hair. "Let's go have some fun." I didn't bother saying goodbye or even looking to see if Rebecca was still there. She showed she wasn't worth my energy by showing her distaste for children. While I'd mentioned I didn't have any, maybe I should have asked if she even liked kids. It didn't seem like it. I was glad I found out now though.

As we walked through the arcade doors and the noise hit us, Benjie tugged on my hand. "That lady wasn't very nice."

"No, she wasn't."

My phone rang, and I quickly pulled it out of my pocket, seeing Dustin's name flash up on the screen. "It's your dad."

Benjie brightened. "Can I talk to him?"

"Of course. Hang on. Hello?"

"Hey, darlin'."

My stomach tingled, and of course my mind took me back to the conversation in the kitchen.

"Here's Benjie," I blurted and thrust the phone at his son.

"Daddy. Hi…. No, we just got out of the movie and now we're in the arcade…. I'll try and let her win." He giggled. "What else has happened? Well, there was this lady and she asked Miss Brooke out on a date." *Dear God, kid, no, no, no.* Yet, when I reached for the phone, Benjie skipped out of the way. "What? Oh no, Miss Brooke said no because she's gonna be busy with me." He lowered his voice to say, "Daddy, the lady didn't seem nice…. Yep, okay, I'll put her on. Bye, Daddy…. Love you too."

I cleared my throat, my hand shaking slightly when I took the phone from Benjie. "H-Hello?"

"Brooke, Brooke, Brooke."

"Benjie, take this money and go get some tokens. But don't go anywhere else and come right back here. I'll be able to see you from here."

"Yep." He took the money and skipped off to wait in line, turning back to smile and wave at me.

"I didn't mean for that to happen in front of Benjie."

"Are you bisexual?" He choked, coughed, and quickly added, "Not that you have to tell me. I didn't mean to ask it like that. Jesus."

My eyes widened over the bluntness, and I would have told him it was none of his business, but he seemed just as shocked by his question as I was. Although, did he seriously want to have this conversation now? Shrugging, I told him, "Yes, but I'm not quite sure the relevance my sexuality has. I know I'm looking after your son, and the last thing I want is for Benjie to hear someone ask me out, male or female, but—"

"Brooke, I don't care Benjie heard. But let me get this straight. You have more of a chance to be asked out by both sexes?"

My head jerked back, confused and a little shocked. "Yes?" I said hesitantly, only it sounded like a question.

His sigh was very audible. "Go out with me?"

I choked on my own saliva. "What?"

"Will you go on a date with me?"

Was he insane?

We couldn't do that. If things went bad, I wouldn't be able to see Benjie again, and that meant more to me than Dustin and his good looks, his sweet body, his charming and funny personality…. No, staying as we were was better. I couldn't be distracted by *him*.

"No."

"Brooke—" A voice in the background called his name. "Fuck, I have to go, but we're not done discussing this, darlin'."

"We are." We had to be, or I feared I'd cave, and I couldn't let that happen.

"Brooke—"

"Benjie's coming back. I have to go."

"Talk soon, darlin'."

Ending the call, I dropped the phone back in my bag and shook my head. There was no way I would talk to Dustin about going on a date. That was crazy.

Why would he suddenly ask me in the first place?

It didn't make sense.

I wasn't his type.

Also, he'd gone out with another woman right in front of me.

He was crazy.

Benjie approached. "Ready?"

"I am, but what was that you were saying about you trying to let me win? Be prepared to lose, sucker."

A giggle bubbled out of him. "I'm not the one who's gonna lose, Miss Brooke."

Taking his hand, I led him over to some machines. "We'll see."

"What were you and Daddy talking about?" Talk about a quick change in subject.

"Just how the movie was."

"Oh, okay."

The rest of the afternoon we played about ten different games and then went to lunch at a burger place. By the time we made it back home, Emily was already there. She must have heard us pull up outside because as we approached, she stepped out with the phone to her ear.

"Yes, they're here." She waved to me as Benjie ran to her for a hug. "Okay, I'll put her on."

Drawn brows, I asked, "Who is it?"

Her lips twitched. "Dustin."

Crap.

He'd called a couple of times as I drove, but I didn't answer, and luckily my car was an old one and there was no Bluetooth in it, so Benjie couldn't see his name flashing.

"Hello?" I stepped away as Benjie told his mom all about our day.

"Darlin', go on a date with me?"

Turning my back on the others, I scrubbed a hand over my face. "No, thank you. I have to go. Bye."

Facing them, I noticed Benjie had disappeared and only Emily was there. I handed her back the phone. "I should get going." I prayed she didn't ask what that conversation was about, or I would feel more awkward than I already did. What was he thinking asking me out again while I was at his ex's house?

"Thank you again. It sounds like he had a lot of fun."

Smiling, I nodded. "We both did."

Benjie flashed around a corner down a hallway and bolted into my legs. "Thank you, Miss Brooke. I hope I get to see you soon."

Leaning down, I kissed his forehead. "I'm sure we'll see each other soon." I just hoped I wouldn't see his father. With another quick goodbye, I made my way back to my car and climbed in just as my phone started ringing.

Picking it up, I sighed and hit the End button.

Didn't he realize there was too much at stake for us to go on a date? My heart for one, and the fact I would miss Benjie. I knew this even after a few times with the little guy. All right, maybe I was holding Benjie in front of me as a shield to protect my heart because I was sure Dustin had the power to crush it. Starting the car, I figured Dustin would eventually get bored with asking me, even though I wasn't sure why he started in the first place. Besides, I was sure he would have many other women to hassle or take out.

CHAPTER SIX

DUSTIN

*E*ven a few days later, I still couldn't get the thought of Brooke dating someone out of my head. When Benjie had mentioned it, a damn furnace had lit in my gut, and I knew, I fucking knew, I hated the thought of her with someone else.

That blazing heat doubled when I realized she had more of a chance of finding someone than anyone else I'd been attracted to. And hell, I was attracted to Brooke. I couldn't deny the attraction and the fact I didn't only want to be friends.

Usually when discovering a woman I was hooking up with was bisexual, it would turn me the hell on thinking of all the fun we could have between the sheets, *if* she was open to bringing another woman into the bedroom. Yet it hadn't with Brooke because I didn't want to share her with *anyone*.

The possessiveness had surprised me, and it seemed had gotten me into trouble when I blurted my invitation out, asking Brooke on a date.

She'd refused to take my calls, and the only texts she responded to were ones that were about Benjie. I was suddenly jealous of my own child. Though I couldn't blame her; my kid was the best.

Me: **Benjie's wondering when he could see you again?**

When she hadn't texted back within five minutes, my mind started rolling with thoughts. *Was she on a date? Who was she with? I'm going to kick whoever's ass she's with. Is she in the shower? Naked? Of course, she's naked in the shower. It's too early to be asleep. Maybe she's tripped and hurt herself. Should I call? Do I need to send an ambulance? She's likely to get pissed if I do and nothing is wrong. Why doesn't she want to date me?*

I sounded like a whiny little bitch, but it had been like that since the phone call, and I really couldn't keep her off my mind. She was there when I went to sleep and when I woke up.

Shit, maybe I needed to see a doctor about my new obsession.

When my phone chimed, I spun back to the coffee table, tripped, and landed on my face. Thank fuck no one was around to see.

Brooke: **If you have something to do tomorrow afternoon, I could come watch him then.**

Did I have anything to do? No.

Me: **Great, I'll let him know.**

Brooke: **Did you have something to do?**

Me: **Say about 4pm? He'll be home from school by then.**

Brooke: **4 is good, but do you have plans?**

My plans were to stick around and spend time with her myself.

Me: **See you then.**

Brooke: **DUSTIN, I SWEAR TO GOD IF YOU ASK ME OUT AGAIN, I WILL CHOP YOUR BALLS OFF!**

At least she was thinking of my balls.

Me: **We haven't even been on a date and you're already talking about my balls.**

Brooke: **I give in.**

My heart skipped a beat.

Me: **Meaning you'll go on a date with me?**

Brooke: **NO. I give in on your stupidity.**

Me: **It's a start to our relationship at least.**

Brooke: **You need help.**

Me: **Are you offering?**

Brooke: **I'm not texting anymore.**

Me: **Because you're too excited to see me tomorrow?**

Me: **The silence tells me you are.**

Me: **It's okay, darlin', just one more sleep and my balls can be yours.**

Me: **Night, Brooke. Looking forward to tomorrow.**

Just as I sent that text, my phone rang. My hopes lifted into a flurry of excitement, only it crashed down when I saw Emily's name on there.

"Hey, Em, you all right?" I may have sounded a little deflated, but my hope had just been burst, damn it.

Her laughter swept through the phone. "Gee, don't sound so excited to hear from me."

Smiling, I offered, "Sorry, I thought you were Brooke."

"Is she still not talking to you?"

"Only in text. But she's coming here tomorrow to see Benjie."

"I'm sure you'll win her over."

"We'll see." Goddamn, I hoped I could.

"What I called for was to see if you mind that I ask Brooke to watch Benjie this weekend? I know you have an away game, but Micky invited me on a weekend away and…."

"You want to go away for a dirty weekend?"

"Well, yes. Is that bad? I shouldn't, should I? That's not being a very good mom when it's my weekend with him. Oh God, now I feel like a terrible mother."

Chuckling, I stood and headed for the kitchen. I'd have to go to bed soon for my ass-crack-of-dawn workout. "Honey, it's fine. How many times have I switched things up on you? The answer is heaps. I'm sure Brooke would love to have Benjie. I might even keep him here and have her stay over. I'll check with her tomorrow. Is that enough notice though?"

"It will be. Thanks for understanding, Dustin."

"Always. We'll talk soon."

"Okay, and good luck with getting Brooke to date you."

"Thanks." I had no doubt I would need it.

Opening the front door, I smiled at a glaring Brooke. "Good afternoon, darlin'." I moved back for her to enter. She must have come directly from work because she was still dressed in pants and a shirt. Items that fitted her curves perfectly. My hands itched to reach out and run over her, but I would probably get a black eye if I did.

She didn't move into the house. Instead, she crossed her arms over her chest, which pushed up her breasts and caused my dick to throb.

Fuck.

"Where's Benjie?"

"He's just getting out of his uniform." I gestured into the house with a wave of the hand.

She scraped her top teeth over her bottom lip before stepping through, bringing her sweet scent with her.

Brooke made her way down the hall and dropped her bag to the floor. The way the pants clung to her ass made me want to become a poet all of a sudden.

How could I have been so blind to her from the start?

I was a fucking fool, that was how.

"Em rang last night. She's in a pickle and is hoping you could help out."

"Oh, how?"

"It's her weekend again with Benjie, but she's wanting to go away with her new beau, and since I have an away game, she was wondering if you're not busy, would you watch Benjie?"

A small soft smile lifted her lips. "Of course I will."

"You are the best, Brooke. Would you be able to stay here so he's not out of place too much?"

"Here?"

"Yeah."

"*Here?*"

"Yes."

"In your house?"

"That's what I was thinking."

"Do you have a spare room?"

"I have a study with no bed in it. But you can just sleep in mine."

"Yours?"

"Yeah."

"*Your bed?*"

My lips twitched when a blush rose in her cheeks. "Darlin', are you okay?"

She coughed, choked, and nodded before she gave me the thumbs-up with both thumbs.

"You're good with staying here?"

"Sure." It sounded a little squeaky.

"You really are a lifesaver, Brooke."

She snorted. "Or I just don't have a life."

I could change that. She could join ours because we're full of life. "Well—"

Her hand shot up with her palm out flat. "Don't."

Grinning, I moved around her to the couch. "Want to sit down?"

Her eyes narrowed. "Don't you have somewhere you need to be?"

"Nope." I sat on the couch and grabbed the remote to switch on the television. "I thought we could watch a movie together."

"Dustin—"

"Miss Brooke!" was yelled from down the hall, and I heard

Benjie's pitter-patter of feet as he ran into the living room and dove at Brooke. She swung him up in her arms with the brightest smile I had seen yet. My heart stuttered and then raced before my body warmed. Benjie cupped her cheeks. "You're here."

"I am. It's good to see you, kiddo." She planted a kiss on his cheek and hugged him close before placing him back on his feet. Benjie took her hand and pulled her to the couch. He sat next to me with Brooke close to him.

"Daddy got a movie for us to watch, and he said we could cook some popcorn."

"Sounds great."

I didn't miss the glare she sent me over Benjie's head. I smirked in response. When I shot her a wink, she looked away.

One day I would win her over. While I'd fucked up, it had been an honest mistake of me being an idiot. I wouldn't do it again.

My phone on the coffee table started ringing and I cringed when Letta's name popped up. I quickly glanced to Brooke to see if she'd seen and caught her looking away from it as her jaw clenched.

"Daddy, you going to answer it?"

Fuck no, I wasn't. I hadn't heard from her since I'd taken her out that day and I didn't want to know what she needed.

Ruffling his hair, I shook my head. "Nah, buddy. It's not important like this movie and the company I have."

"Can we have popcorn now then?"

Chuckling, I stood. "Yeah. Who wants a drink as well?"

"Me," Benjie sang.

Brooke cleared her throat. "I'm fine, thanks."

"I'll be back."

"Do you want us to pause it?" Brooke asked.

Smiling, I moved around the couch. "I'm sure I can catch up." My phone rang again. Letta. Shifting back to the coffee table, I picked it up and turned it off. "Can't have anyone interrupting our movie night."

Benjie beamed up at me before he leaned into Brooke, who put her arm around him. It was no wonder Benjie warmed up to Brooke straight away; she was easygoing, fun, and sweet. He could probably tell she loved the times she was there for him, and in a way, it was good she'd spent time with Benjie first so they could have that bond.

Halfway through the movie, I got up to make some dinner for us and heard someone come into the kitchen a few moments after.

Glancing over my shoulder, I was surprised it was Brooke willing to venture into a room with only me in it.

It was progress at least.

"Do you need some help?"

"What happened to the movie?"

She shrugged and shifted from one foot to another. "We decided to wait for you this time."

Nodding, I smiled. "Sure, I could use some help. Do you want to cut up the lettuce and tomatoes? It's only an easy dinner of tacos."

She walked over to the counter. "I can do that."

As I went back to cooking the meat, I kept flicking my gaze to Brooke not far from me. I liked this. Both of us together in the kitchen cooking. Emily had always hated when I tried to help because she was set in the ways she liked dishes, but having someone help was good.

"How was work today? No glory hole incidents?"

She laughed. "No, thank God. It wasn't too bad. I met Carter's family Tuesday."

"Carter mentioned they got everyone together before he had to go to LA. I'll be leaving Saturday to meet up with him. He didn't say much though. How do you think it went?"

"Good." She smiled over at me. I hadn't had a damn tingle in my gut in a long time. "Reagan finally realizes her feelings for Carter are reciprocated. Oh, and Carter's ex, who works with Reagan and me, followed me to their place after she found out about the family dinner."

Laughing, I shook my head. "Serious?"

"Yep. They quickly got rid of her though."

"Sounds eventful."

"I also got to meet Courtney and State. They invited me to the biker compound when they have their next party."

The spatula dropped out of my hand and hit the floor.

"What?" I demanded a little curtly.

Brooke's brows scrunched down as she looked at the spatula, then up at me. "I'm going to the next party at the compound."

Like fuck she was. "You shouldn't. They get pretty rowdy."

Brooke snorted, shaking her head, and went back to cutting. "I can take care of myself."

Shit. Shit. Shit.

"Excuse me for a moment." I turned down the heat and speed walked into the living room, snatching up my phone.

"Dinner will be ready soon. I've just got to make a call, buddy."

"Okay." He didn't even bother looking up from his comic.

Down near the front door, I put the phone to my ear and waited for State to answer. I'd known Carter for a while, so we knew each other's families, and State and I got along. I'd even been to a couple of parties at the compound myself, which was how I knew they got rowdy.

"Yo, Dusty, what's up?"

"State, love you like a brother, man, but do not invite Brooke to a party at the compound."

He chuckled. "You got a hard-on for her or something? Afraid a brother will hit her up and win her over?"

"You could say that. Look, I fucked up at the start with her, but eventually she'll be mine."

"Good to hear, but I can't not invite her, man. Court and she hit it off, so it'll be outta my hands in the end anyway."

"Fuck." I scrubbed a hand over my hair. "Fine, can you do me a favor and let me know when it's going to happen?"

"Let me guess, you'll want an invite also?"

"You got it."

"All right, man, I can do that."

"You're the best."

"But… if she doesn't want you there, I'll kick you the fuck out."

"What? Why?"

"Win her over quickly, man, because if Brooke's upset you're there, it'll make my old lady upset, and that shit just doesn't happen if I can help it."

"It'll be fine," I reassured him and prayed I wasn't lying.

"It'd better be. Talk soon."

"Got it." With that crisis averted, somewhat, I made my way down the hall and prayed once more that whenever the party would be, I'd be available to go. If not, I'd have to buy Brooke panties with a lock and key on it, and I'd make sure to keep the key, because those brothers at the Diamond MC were horny fuckers.

CHAPTER SEVEN

BROOKE

*A*s I stared down at the bed before me, my stomach ignited with those darn butterflies. How was I supposed to sleep in Dustin's bed without getting lost in his scent like I already was since I walked into his room? I could plug my nose, but I worried I would die in my sleep.

It was already hard enough to keep saying no when he asked me out, but I'd managed to stay strong. There was a chance I'd soften to the idea after sleeping in his scent all night.

He'd said he'd changed his sheets the day before but had to sleep in it last night.

Had he slept naked?

I usually did, but I wouldn't tonight. Especially since Benjie was doors away and could wake up in the middle of the night wanting something. I didn't want to scar the child for the rest of his life. Which was why I was dressed in long pajama pants and a long-sleeved top, an old one I found with the band KISS on it.

Sighing, I pulled my hair up into a makeshift ponytail with my hands and held it there as I stared at the bed some more. I was being ridiculous not climbing in, but I couldn't stop thinking about Dustin between the sheets naked or half naked. To me, bedrooms were sacred. I wouldn't want someone I hardly knew sleeping in my bed. Not where I'd had sex or masturbated.

Wait... how many women had Dustin had in this bed? No, I couldn't think of that. They were fresh sheets, except for one night of Dustin and his masculine scent.

Groaning, I dropped my hands and then scrubbed one over my face.

All I had to remember was that I was here for Benjie. Who cared if Dustin slept right there. If he took his cock in hand and jerked off right *there* on that bed.

Dear God, it suddenly felt very hot in the room.

My phone ringing on the bedside table had me squealing and quickly snatching it up without looking at the screen because I didn't want it to wake up Benjie.

"Hello?"

"Darlin'."

I froze, and an embarrassed noise dropped from my lips. I was standing beside this man's bed, and I'd just been picturing him tugging.

"You all right, sugar?"

"Uh-huh." I nodded to myself as my chest rose and fell

quickly. It was a little too much having him on the phone while I was in his room. I cleared my throat. "Is, ah, something wrong?"

"No, darlin', just ringing to see how the day was." He sounded pleased about something.

"Good. Fine. Great."

His deep chuckle had me closing my eyes to take it in.

"Where are you now?"

My eyes popped open. "Now?"

"Yeah."

"Like, right now?"

Another chuckle rolled through the phone. "I'm guessing you're in my room."

Snorting, I gripped my top at the chest and shook my head. "No. So, um, what are you doing?" I needed to get the conversation off me.

"Just on the bed in the hotel."

Abort. Abort. Abort.

"That's nice." *Nice? Really, Brooke, you went with nice?* "Ah, I should go in case Benjie wakes up." Yet, I couldn't hang up.

Why?

I told Reagan the other day about Dustin and how he'd been asking me out. She mentioned Dustin could be the one, but I brushed off her words, saying he was a player and that if he had been the one, he would have seen a connection or been attracted to me right from the start.

He hadn't, and I couldn't forget that, because if I did, there was a chance I would fall into a world of hurt when he got over whatever infatuation he saw in me. Besides, whatever he did see probably had something to do with how I was with

Benjie. There was a special place in my heart for Benjie because he was such an amazing, sweet, and funny child, who had given me the gift of his trust, and I was more than willing to be his friend and spend time with him. But I wouldn't be more with Dustin because of the connection Benjie and I had. *If* that was all he saw I was good for.

"Brooke…" His tone was soft, sweet, but I wouldn't cave. "Sleep well, darlin'."

"Okay, ah, you too." I quickly ended the call and placed the phone back down.

Since I wasn't going to cave to Dustin, I had to stop being stupid about climbing into his bed.

"Right. I can do this." I nodded to myself before I took the blanket and sheet and flipped them back. Nodding again, I reminded myself, "I'm here for Benjie. Who cares about this bed?" I didn't. Nope. Not at all.

Slipping between the sheets, I dropped my head to the pillow and closed my eyes. If anyone walked in, I probably looked like I was lying in a coffin with how stiff I was. What were my arms doing crossed over my chest?

Drawing in a breath, I relaxed into the mattress more and placed my arms down beside me. Closing my eyes, I ignored the strong scent of Dustin. If I was a creator of perfume, I would bottle his aroma and sell it, knowing I would be a millionaire in a week.

The prick smelled good. Too good.

A stray thought of touching myself crossed my mind, but I stomped on it, kicked it, punched it, and jumped on it before I threw that terrible idea out of my mind.

IT WAS A COUPLE OF WEEKS LATER, WHEN I WAS LOOKING AFTER Benjie again since Emily was out of town on business and Dustin was at an away game, that I had to pick Dustin up from the airport with Benjie. Of course, I took the chance to drive his car to the airport since it was a beast of a thing and needed my attention.

Beside me, Reagan bounced up and down on her feet as the doors opened and the team walked out. Looking down, I caught Benjie watching Reagan—who was officially with Carter, thank God—acting like a loon with a grin on his face. He caught my gaze, and I rolled my eyes with a grin, which had him giggling.

"Carter," Reagan yelled, and she made a mad dash for him.

Laughing, I shook my head at my friend. Not that I could blame her. If I was as in love with someone as she was with Carter, I would have done the same. Heck, I was half in love with him myself because he made my girl so happy. Not only that, but I'd gotten to know his mom well when we had a girls' night, and they were amazing people. Courtney had reminded me again of having a night at the compound, and honestly, I was looking forward to it.

Gently tugging on Benjie's hand, I told him, "Come on, we better follow her, and since she's closer to the group, we might find your dad better."

"Okay." He smiled.

We made our way over, dodging people since it was so busy. Even the paparazzi were there filming the Wolves arriving back in their home state.

We were nearing Reagan and Carter, who were looking lovingly at each other, when I heard, "Benjie."

Benjie's hand slipped from mine as he cried, "Daddy!"

Dustin appeared as Benjie ran the couple of steps and jumped into his dad's arms. They hugged tightly before Dustin placed him back on his feet. "How's my boy?" He grinned down at Benjie, taking his hand.

"Awesome. Miss Brooke took me to the library yesterday after school. I got so many comics it's not funny. We can read them when you're not playing."

"Sounds great, kiddo." He ruffled Benjie's hair before bringing him in close with an arm around his shoulders. Dustin moved his gaze to mine. "Thanks again, Brooke."

Shrugging, I nodded. "Not a problem."

"Dustin, Dustin, who's your lady friend?" a reporter asked.

Another called out, "Benjie, are you proud of your dad getting the winning touchdown?"

"Of course." Benjie beamed.

Dustin suddenly shifted, and a gleam shone in his eyes. Before I could think of doing anything, he'd taken hold of my arm and tugged me into his side. My balance wavered until I placed a hand to his chest and stomach. Both firm. His words had me stilling. "This here is my girlfriend."

He didn't.

He did not just say that aloud to a dang reporter.

Anger ran through my veins. I was going to kill him.

No, I would gut him first and have him beg for mercy before I ended his life.

Shit, I would if he wasn't Benjie's father.

Glaring, I straightened and smacked Dustin in the back of

the head before forcing out a laugh. "He means a girl who is a friend. The trickster." My smile was pinched, my steps away from him were tight, but I had to get away before I punched him in the face.

Reagan, Carter, Dustin, and Benjie caught up to me as we made our way to the baggage claim and out into the multistory parking garage. The whole time I fumed just under the surface and clenched my hands so I didn't throw them around his neck to throttle him.

Nearing our cars, since Reagan and I had followed each other and parked next to one another, I called out to my friend, "Hey, Ree, can you give me a lift home?" Turning, I threw Dustin's keys to him, which he caught. I'd been hoping he'd have his mouth open and he could have choked on them.

"But, Miss Brooke, you said we could build a fortress later." Benjie rushed up to me, wrapped his arms around me, and looked up with a cute little pout on his face.

Smiling softly, I couldn't help but love this kid, and I knew if I went over there, I would murder his father. Running a hand through his hair, I said, "I promise the next time together we'll do it."

"Brooke—"

I shot Dustin a scowl that shut him up, and he thinned his lips and turned to Reagan. "Is that okay?"

Reagan took us all in, and I felt Benjie move back to his dad before she replied, "Sure. Not a problem."

"Kiddo," Dustin said, "can you jump in the car while I have a quick word with Brooke?"

"Sure," Benjie replied with a smile and grabbed the keys from his dad. I'd never seen him move so quickly to the car.

"Ree, let's get in ours," I heard Carter say.

"But—" Knowing my friend, she'd want to have my back or, more importantly, want to know what Dustin wanted to say to me. Not that I wanted to stick around and find out, but I wasn't a total bitch. Besides, I would use this time to give him a good reaming... probably the wrong word to use.

"Sweetheart," Carter tried again.

Reagan sighed. "Fine." She caught my gaze. "If you need help maiming him, just call."

Smiling, I nodded, always grateful for her. Dustin didn't say anything until they were both in the car, and he took a step closer. I stepped back one, nearing the back of Reagan's car.

"What could you possibly have to say now?"

"Sorry?"

My gaze narrowed. "You're not sorry."

His lips pulled up at the corner. "Not really."

"You're unbelievable."

Dustin threw up a hand. "I am sorry it pissed you off, but after seeing you there, I wished what I said wasn't a lie. I want you to be mine, Brooke. I know I fucked up royally that first time you came to my house. I should have taken you, not her. It should have been you all along."

Shaking my head, I rubbed at the side of my neck. "You're crazy. I'm not your type. I'm—"

He was in front of me, a hand threading through my hair, the other to my waist. "You are my type, Brooke. I can't get you off my mind." His lips were on mine. I tried to pull back, but he followed and we knocked into the car. I pushed at his arms, but when his tongue swept over my bottom lip, I caved and gave into my heart as it beat rapidly for him.

I kissed him back.

It was hard, hot, and demanding... but too quickly my brain caught up with my actions.

Tearing my mouth from his, I pushed him back. "We can't." I stomped to the passenger door to Reagan's car, opened it, and slid in, closing it after me.

"Can you believe that idiot? Carter, do me a favor and run over him as you back out."

He snorted and started the car. "Not sure the team would be happy with me."

Rolling my eyes, I fixed my shirt and explained, "But we'd be happy, and Ree will make you even happier if you helped her BFF out. Won't you, Ree?"

Please say yes so he can run him over.

"I'd make him happy even if he ran Dustin over or not."

"Some friend you are." I glanced out the back of the window and watched as Dustin moved to my window. "Damn, he's moved." If he thought I would roll it down, he could think again.

But that kiss—

Shut the hell up.

He bent with a big stupid grin on his face. It annoyed me so much I gave him the middle finger. His response was to wink as he said, "Talk soon, darlin.'"

No, we wouldn't.

"Can we go?" I snapped at Carter in the driver seat.

Carter backed out while Dustin moved to his car and got in.

Dear God, had Benjie seen? What would he think? I swore if Benjie saw and got his hopes up, I would castrate Dustin.

When I voiced my worries, Reagan reassured me he hadn't seen, and a wave of relief rolled over me, since Benjie had started talking to me about how awesome his dad was, and I had a feeling he was trying to hint at me dating him.

But for Benjie's sake and my own, I couldn't let that happen.

But that kiss—

Yes, all right, I could admit it was everything I thought it would be. It ignited my body from the top of my head to the bottom of my feet. My lips still hummed from the contact. My body still craved more.

That was another reason Dustin and I couldn't get involved. He drew out more in me than any other person had. Female and male.

He had the power to wreck me, and I didn't know if I could let that happen.

Growling under my breath, I rubbed my hand over my face. I didn't know what was best, but that kiss kept playing over and over in my head.

When Reagan and Carter dropped me off, I realized I'd left my car at Dustin's. Reagan said she'd pick me up the next day for work, but I still had to face Dustin to get my car and wasn't sure if I would punch him or kiss him.

CHAPTER EIGHT

BROOKE

*M*iss Baker."

I jolted from my daze as I walked down the school's hallway toward my office. It was too early for anything, but I still turned to Jenifer, who had whispered my name in a snappish tone.

"Yes, Jenifer?"

She moved over close and glanced around us. It was early enough not many students littered the hallways.

I really needed another coffee.

"Um, there's like a heap of flowers in your office."

Stopping, I looked at her as she nodded. "A heap?"

"A ton."

Murder would be too good for Dustin.

Picking up my pace, I stalked through the halls until I

reached the hallway where my office sat in the middle, and already I could see flowers sticking out of the open doorway. Whoever unlocked my office door for this was going to get my foot up their ass.

"See, there's heaps," Jenifer said when we reached the doorway. I hadn't even noticed she was still with me. But she was right, there were heaps. Literally every surface was covered in bunches of different types of flowers. Even my floor.

The door across from me opened, and Stinky Steve, the physical education teacher, stepped out. "Oh, hey, Brooke. Hope you don't mind I got Frank the janitor to open your room for the delivery."

Slowly, I faced him and caught his eyes widening before he took a step back.

"Someone must be really sorry, Miss Baker," Jenifer commented, but I was too busy killing Steve with my mind.

"All right, got to go." Steve jogged down the hall, and that was when I noticed Tom coming my way.

"Shit." Panicking, because I knew he would ask questions I didn't want to answer, I shoved and shut the door before turning and leaning against it.

Tom's steps faltered and then stopped right in front of me. "Brooke."

"Morning, Tom. Great day, isn't it?"

His gaze narrowed. "What have you done?"

"Moi." I touched my chest and acted surprised as I used the only French word I knew. "Why, I've done nothing."

A knock sounded.

"Miss? Can I come out? I have to get ready for class."

Fuck my life.

Tom crossed his arms over his chest. "Who was that?"

"Who was what?" I countered, looking up and down the hall.

"Brooke."

"Tom. Glad we can remember each other's names."

He sighed and scrubbed a hand over his face. "I swear to God, I need therapy just to deal with you and Reagan."

"Miss Baker, sorry, but I don't like to be late."

Goddamn goody two-shoes.

Tom's brow rose.

Thinning my lips, I moved to the side and opened my door to let Jenifer out. I hadn't even noticed I'd pushed her in there in my panicked state.

"What in the f— Jenifer, you had better get to class."

I would have laughed when Jenifer bowed at the principal, but I was honestly concerned that Tom's gaze didn't move from my office.

"Bye, Miss Baker."

"Later, Jenifer, and sorry about shutting you in there."

She smiled. "It's okay."

As soon as she started moving, I stepped into my office and went to close the door. Tom's hand landed on it and held it open.

"What's all this? Did someone upset you? Who was it? Herb and I'll kick his ass. We might look charming, but we can be deadly."

My heart expanded with those mushy, sweet feelings. Tom had always been a little more lenient with Reagan and me because we'd known each other for a while, even before we started working here, since Tom and Herb were friends.

"It was Dustin."

I waited.

Knew it was coming.

Tom's face blanked. He cleared his throat. "Yes, ah, well, they have the Super Bowl coming up, so Herb and I'll schedule a beatdown after that for him."

Snorting, I rolled my eyes and smiled.

"Of course."

Turning, I shifted through the flowers and made it to my desk, where a note sat on it. I didn't pick it up; instead, I said to Tom, "Don't worry, I'll get this cleaned up."

"I know you will." He shifted into the room and shut the door.

Shit.

"Can I ask what happened?"

Sighing, I leaned back in the chair. "Short version. He wants to date me, but I won't because he didn't see me from the start, and the biggest problem is if it doesn't work out, I won't get to see his son, Benjie, again. We've become close since I started helping out and minding him."

He gaped at me. "You... he... but you... date him!"

Shaking my head, I pointed at him. "You're only saying that because you're in love with him and his team."

"No. I've followed the Wolves for as long as I can remember. I read up on all the news about them, and you know there's good and bad when a person is in the spotlight. Dustin has been seen as... all right, he's been called a player, but that type of news hasn't happened for the last month." Tom waved a hand around. "Don't know if you've realized, but it looks to me he's been courting you for a long time and you haven't noticed. Obviously, he's sorry about something, but at least he knows he's in the bad books and is willing to try and get out of them. I'm a man—"

"Really?"

"Shut up. I've been lazy in relationships in the past and didn't give two hoots if I hurt a woman's feelings. I doubt Dustin did either. Until you."

Why did he have to go and say crap like that?

Straightening, I rested my elbows on the desk. "It doesn't matter. I'm not risking anything because of Benjie."

"Aren't Dustin and his ex good friends? Dustin wouldn't do anything to risk hurting his son in any way."

Glaring, I pointed toward the door. "Quit making sense and get out."

Tom snorted. "What did he do anyway? Was it bad?"

"Yes! He kissed me."

Tom gasped and clutched his chest. "That bastard." He rolled his eyes and turned, moving back to the door. "Don't wipe the idea away, Brooke."

"You just want me to date him because he's on the Wolves and you'll see more of him."

At the door, Tom turned and shook his head. "I want you to give him a chance because I think he could make you happy, and that's really what I want. To see you happy."

He was gone before I could say or do anything since I'd melted into a puddle of goo. I wasn't sure how I got so lucky with the people in my life, but I really had. It didn't mean I'd stop from giving Tom shit all the time.

Grazing my bottom lip with my top teeth, I glanced down to the note and picked it up. I pulled it free from its little envelope and read it.

Brooke, I'll always be sorry for what happened that first time, but never that kiss. One chance, darlin'. Just one and I'll prove myself to you.

My hand shook as I placed the note back down. Pressing my fist to my stomach to try and settle the butterflies, I closed my eyes and scrunched up my face.

Why did the asshole have to be sweet? That shit shot me right in the chest, but I couldn't wipe away my fear that if it didn't last, Benjie would get hurt.

Was my happiness more important than Benjie?

No. I didn't believe it was.

WHEN IT REACHED FRIDAY, I STILL HADN'T SENT A TEXT TO Dustin thanking him for the over-the-top gift of flowers. I'd pushed it aside since I'd been pissed it'd taken me all day to clean that shit up. But then I didn't know what to say, because half of me didn't want to lead him on by thanking him, but the other half wanted me to run to his house naked and kiss him again while I humped his leg. That side was a lot sluttier than I actually was.

Guilt had me sitting in my car out front of Dustin's because I hadn't said anything to him, even after the few texts and calls he'd tried with me.

I wasn't a complete bitch. I did feel bad when I knew I was being a childish dickhead.

Nerves swept through me like my blood did in my veins, but I climbed out of the car and flung my bag over my shoulder.

Just don't kiss him.

I wasn't supposed to need to remind myself that, but Dustin was always on my mind, and I kept running over the thought of giving in and dating him. I wanted him. I did, but boy, was I scared. Which translated to me that I wasn't ready to risk my heart or Benjie and be selfish to give in to what I wanted. Which was Dustin's mouth on mine.

On the walk up to the door, my nose started twitching and I knew it was one of those pesky nostril hairs tickling me. I rubbed at it, but it kept annoying me. Glancing around, I saw no one, and quickly stuck the tips of two fingers up there, ready to pull that nuisance free… when the door opened.

Dustin grinned. "Never thought I'd open the door to a gorgeous woman picking her nose."

Heat hit my cheeks and I dropped my hand, but it tickled again so I rubbed the side of it. "I wasn't. There's a hair tickling me."

"Uh-huh."

"It's true." I rubbed it again on the outside and finally there was sweet relief. It must have moved.

His lips twitched. "Sure."

Can I just die, please?

"I'm going now."

Turning, I heard his chuckle before my upper arm was taken in a firm grip and I was spun back to face him.

"Darlin', you ain't going anywhere." I was surprised he removed his hand and took a step back. "Come on in."

"I—"

"Please."

Biting my bottom lip, I nodded and stepped through, making my way down into the living room. "Is Benjie not with you today?"

"Not until next week."

Well, shit. I liked having a buffer between us.

Quickly, I sat on one end of the couch and dropped my bag to the floor. I bounced my leg up and down as I watched him take the other end of the couch with a smirk. It was better than bouncing on him.

Do not think of that.

"So, I, ah...."

"You're not usually nervous around me, darlin'."

Narrowing my eyes, I pointed at him. "It's your damn fault with that stupid kiss." I blanched. I actually felt the color drain from my face. I hadn't meant to say that. His smirk grew into a grin.

"Why are you here, darlin'?"

Looking away from him, I glanced at the game on the television and noted it must have been an old one because Dustin was on the screen. I quickly looked elsewhere. "I just wanted to drop in to see Benjie and say thank you for the flowers. They were a bit too much, but I appreciate them."

My gaze spun back when I felt him shift closer. "You're welcome. I didn't think you liked them since I hadn't heard from you."

Nodding, I cleared my throat and stared at his knees. They were good knees.

Crap, maybe he thought I was looking at his crotch. I

averted my gaze to the coffee table and thankfully my phone picked that moment to ring. I prayed it was a lifeline out of this awkward situation.

Dipping my hand into my bag, I pulled it out and saw Nana Bev's name on the screen. "Sorry, I have to take this."

"Not a problem."

"Nana, is everything okay?"

"Why you gotta ask that? It's like you think somethin' is gonna be wrong every time I ring. Like I've fallen down and can't get up. Child, my legs are still strong. They can still hold a man's hips between them, or head, if I wanna get freaky like that."

Dropping my head, I sighed.

Why couldn't she have a normal conversation?

When Dustin chuckled beside me, I knew, just *knew*, he had heard everything she said.

"Oooh, boo, whose sweet voice is that in the background? Wait, are you on a date? Are you gettin' some, child?"

"Nana, why would I answer the phone if I was getting some?"

Why, dear God, did I ask that? I could have tit punched myself.

"Love you with all my heart, boo, but sometimes you do weird shit. Now tell your nana who that voice belongs to. Have you told him you can't cook? Tell him he better pray to Jesus when he eats anything you make."

"Nana, I have to go—"

"Not before—"

"I'm on my way to your place now and we can talk."

"Child, do not move from wherever you are. Not when a

man is there and laughing in that rich, dark voice. Can you imagine what his bedroom voice sounds like?"

"Bye!" I yelled before I ended the call. I dropped the phone to the couch and covered my face with my hands. "Can we pretend you didn't hear any of that?"

Dustin chuckled again, and Nana was right... it was dark and rich.

"Not a chance, sweetheart."

Standing, I grabbed my bag. "Anyway, I better go. Nice seeing you. Catch up soon." I headed for the doorway.

"You don't want to stay for a drink?"

"Nope, got to go." I waved over my shoulder, not that I was sure he followed. I opened the front door and closed it quickly in case he was on his way, then bolted for my car like the chicken shit I was.

CHAPTER NINE

DUSTIN

*S*till smiling, I made my way back down the hall after watching Brooke fly out of here like her pants were on fire. I didn't think she needed to be embarrassed over the phone call. Hell, I wanted to meet her nana because she was hilarious.

The woman consumed all my thoughts. Even Carter and North noticed how I'd changed. I used to flirt with the women who fawned over the team, but now it was like they were nothing. I wanted more. I wanted someone to come home to. Someone who would come to my games. Someone I could call my own. And I wanted that person to be Brooke. My gut spun at the idea of finally having her, and what I wanted with her wasn't just for one night or a weekend or even a month. I wanted her forever.

Usually, a thought like that had me gagging, but it didn't when I imagined it with Brooke.

Just as I entered the living room, a phone rang, and it wasn't my usual ringtone. Moving over to the couch, I realized Brooke had left her phone behind. At least it would give me an excuse to see her again.

Since I was interested in seeing who was ringing, I picked it up and saw Nana Bev's name. It wouldn't be very nice of me if I didn't let her nana know Brooke left her phone.

Smiling, I swiped the screen and put the phone to my ear. "Brooke's phone."

"My oh my, and who do we have here?"

My smile widened. "My name's Dustin Grant, ma'am."

"Dustin, do you have my granddaughter busy there?" I wanted to laugh at how hopeful she sounded.

"No, ma'am, she accidentally left her phone. I think she's on her way to you anyway."

"Dang it, I wanted her to pick up some bourbon for me. Anyway," she drew out. "Can I ask what the relationship is between you and my granddaughter?"

"Currently, we're friends, but I'm trying to... woo her."

She hummed under her breath. "And how long have you known her? What do you do for a living? How much money do you have in your bank account? What blood type are you?"

Laughing, I shook my head. "I've known Brooke for a while now. My son, Benjie—"

Her gasp had me stilling. She coughed and exclaimed, "You're the douche-bucket who took another woman out on a date when my grandbaby was available?"

Fuck.

"Yeah, that was me, and I regret it with my whole damn heart."

"She adores your boy, you know. Every time I talk to her, it's all she can talk about."

"I know she does." The thought of Brooke with Benjie, how patient and sweet she was with him, warmed me.

"Are you doin' other women?"

I choked at her bluntness. "No, ma'am."

"You want my Brooke?"

"I do."

"She may come across as a hardass sometimes, but knowing her, she wouldn't want anythin' with you because of the risk of your boy."

"What I'm looking for with her isn't a short-time thing."

She hummed under her breath again. "On Fridays she comes to my place for dinner."

What was I supposed to say to that? "That's, ah, nice."

"I think you should come also."

I grinned. "I'd like that, ma'am."

"Good. Don't tell her. Let it be a surprise."

"My lips are sealed."

"You'd better treat my grandbaby right, Dustin Grant. If you don't, no matter how your voice sounds, I'm still young enough to kick your ass."

"I will, ma'am."

"Call me Nana Bev, boy." She rattled off her address and then hung up. What we'd planned may have been a little deceitful, but I was willing to do anything to get Brooke to see I was serious and that she needed to trust me. If Nana Bev was willing to help me, then I'd take it.

Nana Bev opened the door and looked me over before she stepped back and waved me in with "You'll do."

Chuckling, I stepped into the house and closed the door for her. "It's nice to actually meet you, Nana Bev." I handed her the bunch of flowers in my hand.

"Boy, you don't need to charm my panties off, just my Brooke's."

Jesus. Another chuckle left me as she shuffled down further into the living room.

"She should be here any moment." She moved over to the table in the joined dining room and dropped the flowers into an empty vase on it. Turning to me, she added, "I'll put water in them in a moment, but I wanna see Brooke's reaction." A glint shone in her eyes as she rubbed her hands together. "Take a seat." I walked to the couch facing the dining room. "No, not there. This one over here so she can see you right away."

My brows shot up, but I did as I was asked, well... ordered, since I didn't think arguing with her was the best choice if I wanted to live.

Nana Bev moved around the couch I sat on and slowly sat at the other end. She eyed me like I was a puzzle she was trying to piece together.

"You're young. Are you sure you're done screwin' around?"

Holy shit, her bluntness, once again, had me choking on my own saliva. "Yes, definitely sure." No other woman caught my eye like Brooke had. Once I'd got my head out of my ass.

"I need great-grandbabies, and Brooke is still young. Are you wanting more kids?"

Kids with Brooke?

Oh shit, I shivered at the idea of Brooke's rounded belly with *my* child in it.

Nana Bev cackled. "I'll take that moony look as a yes."

A car door slammed out front. Nana Bev and I glanced to the front door. Brooke opened it and stepped in, calling, "Nana Bev—" Her eyes widened, her mouth dropped open, and heat hit her cheeks. Brooke's bag slipped from her shoulder and dropped to the floor. Her phone fell out, the one I'd taken into her work for her, to which she kicked me right back out after a quick thank-you.

"Look, Boo, I have a guest."

Brooke's gaze narrowed in on her grandmother. I was glad it wasn't directed at— Too late, she'd turned it on me.

"What are *you* doing here?"

"Nana Bev invited me for dinner." I grinned and stood.

Brooke took a step back.

"Boo, you know I love you, but I'm thinking you need to give this nice young man a chance. He's promised me he's over his hookin' days—"

"Not that I was ever a hooker." I wanted to clear that up.

Nana Bev rolled her eyes. "It's time you put your worries aside, Brooke. This handsome man wants you to take a chance on him, and from what I'm seein', it could be good for the both of you."

"I... he... no." She shook her head and scowled at both of us. Her walls were up. If I was in her shoes and someone was telling me to do something, I'd have my back up too. Suddenly, I wasn't sure this night was a good idea.

Nana Bev's lips thinned. "How about we just have dinner then?"

Brooke's gaze flicked to me and back to her grandmother. "All of us?"

"Yes. I invited Dustin here when he and I spoke, after you left your phone at his place. I wanted to get to know the father of the boy you adore."

Brooke scrunched her nose up, and I was sure she was about to tell me to take a hike, until she sighed. "All right."

"Good. I'll finish up in the kitchen and yell when it's done."

"I can help," Brooke offered.

Nana Bev laughed. "Thanks, but no. I want dinner edible." With my help, she stood and made her way through the dining room into the kitchen.

Brooke shuffled her feet. "How's Benjie?"

"He's good."

She nodded. "That's great."

"I can leave if you want me to." *Please say no.*

She shrugged. "Nana would kill me if I got rid of her eye candy for the night."

"Damn right" was yelled from the kitchen.

Grinning, I scratched at my cheek. "You think I'm eye candy?"

Brooke snorted as she picked up her bag and walked over to the couch. She placed her bag on the coffee table and sat. I quickly sat at the other end. "I said she would have thought of you as eye candy, not me."

"Bullshit," Nana Bev coughed out.

Leaning in, I told her, "Your nana is awesome."

Her features softened. "Yeah, she is, but don't tell her that. It'll go to her head."

Winking, I nodded. "My lips are sealed. But back to the eye candy part."

Brooke groaned, but I caught her smile. "You know you're good-looking, Dustin."

"Maybe, but do *you* like what you see?"

Another groan, and I wanted to feel it on my lips. Her cheeks pinked, and she looked everywhere but at me. "You're not bad."

"Not bad?" My tone held an edge of offense to it.

She smiled. "Yeah, not bad."

"All right." I nodded. "I can handle that. Not that you'd ask, but I'm completely attracted to you."

Her eyes widened and she quickly glanced to the kitchen where we heard clattering going on. Her lips thinned before she said, "I like the way I look, but Dustin, don't pull my leg, okay. I'm not your usual type."

"Does that matter? Can't you see that my usual type doesn't work for me? I damn well love the way you look, Brooke. Don't question my attraction to you. Shit, I have to try not to embarrass myself when I think of you—"

Crunch. Crunch. Crunch.

Brooke and I both looked behind us to see Nana Bev in the doorway eating some potato chips. "What? This stuff is gettin' good."

"Dear God." Brooke buried her face in her hands. She stood and pointed at me. "That conversation can happen at another time... like never." She looked to her nana. "Is dinner ready?"

"Sure is. Come help me get it to the table. Both of you." She rolled her chip packet up and walked back into the kitchen.

Before Brooke could follow, I took her wrist in hand and turned her toward me, cupping her cheek. Leaning in, my lips caressed her ear. She shivered as I placed my other hand on her waist. "I could tell you about all the times I've thought of you as I jerked off and came quickly because the thought of you naked turns me the fuck on. Never question how attracted I am to you." After a brush of my lips to her cheek, I stepped back and found a dazed look in her eyes. It seemed she was having trouble breathing.

Bopping her on the nose, I smiled, winked, and went into the kitchen.

Nana Bev turned. "Where's Brooke?"

"She needs a moment."

Her eyes narrowed. "Would it be a good or a bad moment?"

I shrugged. "Good, I reckon."

Nana Bev grinned. "All right, boy." She thrust a tray of vegetables at me. "Take this to the table and come back for more."

There wasn't a question about me doing as I was told, since Nana Bev kind of scared me. Brooke ended up helping toward the end and we all sat down for a roast dinner. I knew I'd enjoy the company, but I didn't consider how much. The conversation flowed, the laughter came and went, and Brooke's tension seemed to slip away.

By the time I walked Brooke out to her car after dinner, we both had smiles on our faces.

What I didn't like was when her brows pinched as she faced me when we got to her car. She glanced to my vehicle. "I didn't even see your car parked there."

Reaching out, I tucked some of her stray blonde hair behind her ear. "Too distracted? Did you have a bad day at work?"

She swallowed and shook her head. "No." The word came out softly before she grazed her bottom lip with her top teeth. "Dustin... Benjie."

"We don't have to tell him anything, for now."

"But—"

With my hands landing on her hips, I pulled her into me and waited for her gaze to lift to mine. "Please, Brooke, give this a chance." I'd never wanted anything so bad in my life before. I cocked a brow. "What do you say?"

Another graze to her bottom lip as she looked to the side. "We won't tell Benjie anything until we know it's more than... whatever it'll be?"

"Not a word."

"I, ah, suppose we could go on a few dates to see if we get along."

"We do."

"But there could be something you don't like about me or me about you."

"I doubt it, but I'm happy with a few dates to start with." Forever we could plan together.

She looked to the side. "Okay" was whispered.

"Yeah?"

When her gaze lifted to mine, it was warm. "Yes."

"Please tell me this is date one and that I can kiss you?"

Her face lightened with humor. "I suppose."

I dropped my lips to hers as she wrapped her arms around my neck and lifted to her tippy-toes. Tilting my head, I slid the tip of my tongue inside and she took it, opening her mouth to receive a deeper, hotter kiss.

A moan slipped from her lips and joined with my own groan when I tugged her even closer with my hand curled around her waist. I slid the other hand up to cup the back of her head as the kiss went on in a frenzy of nipping, tasting, and enjoying.

My dick was rock hard, and I knew she felt it when she rubbed up and down against it.

Breaking the kiss, I dropped my forehead to hers and panted along with her. "Fuck, darlin'."

That kiss was better than our first.

That kiss had me wanting it again and again.

That kiss made me want to take her right here and now.

"If I don't stop, your nana will get more of a show."

She snorted out a laugh. "We can't do that."

"No, we can't. When can I take you out?"

She hadn't yet looked away from my lips, reassuring me she wanted more. I would have given it to her, but there was honest concern it'd lead to more. I doubted Nana Bev's neighbors were ready for a private porn show.

"Darlin', you're killing me." With a quick peck to her lips, I stepped back and ran a hand over my face. "When, Brooke?"

"You have that, ah, Super Bowl game coming up. Maybe after that?"

"I'll call you." I smirked. "Will you answer this time?"

She laughed. "Yes."

"Night, darlin'." I gave her a stupid wave, not really wanting to leave.

"Goodnight." Her smile was warm and was all for me.

Goddamn, that made my heart happy.

I nodded to her car. "You're going to have to leave before me. I can't walk away from you right now."

She bit her bottom lip, but the corners of her mouth tipped up. "Talk soon?"

"Yeah, darlin'."

With a nod, she unlocked her car and climbed in. I waited until she drove off down the road before I moved over to my car. I heard the front door open and saw Nana Bev grinning.

"She's agreed to a couple of dates to see how things go."

Nana Bev gave me two thumbs up. "Good job, son."

"Thanks for your help, Nana Bev."

I unlocked my car and had the door open when she called, "Don't fuck this up now or I'll fuck you up, and not in a sexual way."

Chuckling, I shot her a salute and got in my car. Finally, I had my shot with the woman who'd consumed my mind and was going to be my future. Not that she knew. There was no way I was screwing this up.

CHAPTER TEN

BROOKE

*G*ood game," I said into the phone just after I arrived home from the Super Bowl, which they won. My nerves were eating at my stomach lining for reaching out in the first place, but I felt I had to since Dustin had been the one to make all the other calls first.

"Thanks, darlin'. I didn't know you were going to come. I would have liked to have seen you after."

"Reagan needed the support. She tried to jump the rails a few times when Carter got tackled. It's lucky it was his last game for her nerves."

His chuckle had me shivering. "Why doesn't her actions surprise me. Are you at home now?"

"I am. What about you?" Dropping my bag to the stand just inside the living room, I moved over to the couch and sat.

"I wish I was, but there's press shit to do. I appreciate the call, darlin.'"

"Okay." Okay? Why would I say okay? That sounded lame. "Um, before you have to go, Courtney asked me to the Diamond MC compound for a family party night this Friday."

"The compound?"

"Yes, and I was hoping you could come. I mean, you don't have to if you're busy. I'll just go—"

"I'll come," he rushed out before he cleared his throat. "I'm glad you asked. Want me to pick you up?"

"Courtney's already offered."

"All right, darlin.' I'll give you a lift home."

My belly fluttered. "Okay." It seemed "okay" was my go-to word when it came to Dustin. "See you Friday."

"You will, but I'll talk to you before then. Night, darlin.'"

"Goodnight." The smile wouldn't go away, which added a layer of worry as I was happy. While it was like a weight had lifted off my shoulders when I'd finally agreed to date Dustin since I was tired of thinking of the what-ifs, I was scared over the possibility of losing out on something that could be good. That it was a potential relationship where it could really go somewhere.

I doubted the worry would vanish, but I would live with it.

"ARE YOU SURE IT'S OKAY FOR ME TO COME?" I ASKED Courtney again because the compound had been locked down when we'd arrived, until the gatekeeper—yes, they had one—waved us through once the gate opened. Suddenly, I felt like an outsider intruding on something.

Courtney laughed and took my hand, dragging me through the door. "I'm completely sure. You'll love this place and the people in the club. They're really a great group. I'm proud to call them family."

"I believe you, but I'm still worried about being an outsider. Also, there's a chance I could shit myself and possibly vomit from meeting new people. Did I mention I don't do well in crowds? Do you know the last time there was a group of people I mentioned anal beads? This isn't going to go well for you."

Courtney roared with laughter and curled her arm around my shoulders, taking me further into the compound. "Don't worry. There's that type of talking around here. You'll fit right in."

Why did I say I wanted to come? I couldn't remember, especially since I walked into a room filled with boisterous bikers and their partners.

Swallowing thickly, I stopped when Courtney's two children, Caitlyn and Crispin, who I'd met when I went to Reagan and Carter's, came running up. They made me think of Benjie. I hadn't seen him in four days, and I missed the little monster.

"Mommy, Saint told Crispin he can have a beer."

Courtney's arms dropped and her hands went to her hips. "Saint!" She turned to Crispin. "You are not having a beer."

Crispin rolled his eyes. "I know, Mom."

A blond guy behind the bar started laughing, and State

stood by, chuckling with him. Another guy, who had a nice ass, turned, and it seemed the room and my concerns faded.

Dustin stood at the bar until he saw me. He grabbed something off the counter and stalked toward me with a big smile on his face.

"If I wasn't happily married, I would totally be jealous right now."

A girly giggle slipped out of me as I glanced to Courtney and back again. I was lucky, and Dustin looked amazing in his jeans and tee. Casual and yet hot.

"Hey, darlin'." He leaned in and kissed the corner of my mouth. My nipples perked up for his attention.

Courtney made a noise in the back of her throat. "I'm swooning with that voice."

"Dad, Mom's swooning over Mr. Grant," Crispin yelled across the room.

State straightened, and if looks could kill, Dustin would be dead. "Woman, get your sweet ass over here."

"Honey, I wasn't—"

"She was," Crispin supplied loudly.

Courtney grabbed the back of Crispin's neck and covered his mouth. Caitlyn giggled, and I knew Crispin was as well. State stalked our way. I didn't miss the way Dustin slid in behind me.

"I have something for you." He slipped something over my head, then helped me put my arms through the armholes.

Dustin got me a jersey.

Before I could glance down, State stopped in front of Courtney, cupped the back of her head, and kissed her soundly. Crispin, who had gotten out of his mom's hold, gagged, while Caitlyn ran back over to the bar and up into the arms of another man.

When they came up for air, State clipped, "Mine, always."

"Of course," Courtney breathed.

Now it was my turn to swoon.

They looked toward us, and State started roaring with laughter. Courtney covered her mouth to hide her own mirth.

"What?" I asked.

Dustin curled an arm around my shoulders. "Don't worry about them."

But when Courtney pointed at my chest, I looked down and saw wording. I pulled it out and read Grant's Property. I lifted my gaze and caught the words on Courtney's vest. State's Property.

Dustin was claiming me at a biker's compound.

"I don't know if I should be pissed you don't trust me or pleased."

He shifted in front of me, blocking off everyone. "Pleased, darlin', always pleased. It's those assholes"—State grunted as Dustin spoke—"who I love and adore, that I don't trust. They'll hump your leg if you give them a chance—"

"That was one time," a man called, and laughter surrounded us.

My cheeks burned at the realization that more than just State and Courtney were listening.

"Honestly, darlin', it was—"

I covered his mouth with my hand. "I love it." And I did. It actually meant a lot to me and was a sweet gesture. He wanted to make sure people knew I was his. How could I be mad about that? I couldn't.

Lowering my hand, I got to my tippy-toes and gave him a quick kiss. "Thank you."

He smiled brightly. "You're welcome." Shifting to the side, he wound an arm around my waist. "Come on. Let's get you a drink."

Nodding, I grinned down at my jersey and had Dustin lead me toward the bar. Courtney and State followed.

At the bar, I got to meet Saint and his boyfriend Gun, or Kylo, as he said. There was also the president of the Diamond MC, named Country.

Nana Bev would have loved it, as I had to admit I was surrounded by eye candy. Not as good as Dustin, but it was very close.

"What will you have?" Saint asked.

"Vodka and raspberry if you have it."

He winked. "You got it."

"Dustin Grant," a new man said as he stopped beside us. They slapped each other's hands and gave a half hug. "Good game the other night."

It was okay to appreciate good looks, right?

Leaning into Courtney, I muttered, "Is everyone good-looking in this club?"

She laughed. "I thought the same thing the first night I was here." She patted my arm. "Don't worry, you'll see once you're around them longer how annoying they are."

"You wouldn't be talking about me?" Another new man arrived. This one was model material with silky blond hair and cheekbones that made me jealous. He seemed a little younger than others, but age was just a number... and I wasn't supposed to think that.

Courtney snorted. "Never you, West."

A finger tapped under my chin, and I snapped my mouth closed, my cheeks heating when I glanced to Dustin, who'd been the one to tap me.

"I didn't...."

He pulled me in close and kissed my neck. "It's fine. Even a straight guy can tell how good-looking West is."

"Aww, aren't you the sweetest, Dustin." West winked.

"Nyet, I do not think so."

Dustin stiffened as another man moved up behind West and glared at Dustin. Even I wanted to pee myself from the coldness of his gaze.

West only grinned and turned, wrapping his arms around the man's waist. "I only have eyes for you, babe."

"That is good, *moya lyubov'*, because I am not in the mood to kill tonight."

"Why does he sound like he's serious?" I whispered to State next to us.

State chuckled. "Because he is."

Oh. *Oh.* I swallowed thickly. If he hadn't looked down to West with such adoration in his eyes, I would have run for the hills. But it was there for everyone to see, which calmed my racing pulse.

West's sweet smile turned to us. "Hi, I'm West, and this is my partner, Adrik."

"I'm Brooke, and Dustin is cowering behind me."

Dustin huffed, his arms round my waist tightening. "I wouldn't say cowering, exactly."

West waved him off. "Don't worry, Adrik wouldn't actually kill you—"

"Do not say things that are not true, moya lyubov'. For you, I will kill."

Yep, he really sounded serious.

The other man who'd greeted Dustin rolled his eyes and snorted. "Enough killin' talk. I got enough shit to deal with without havin' a brawl in the bar."

"Death, this is Brooke," Dustin said.

Death?

Why would he have a club name of Death?

"Um, hi," I squeaked.

"Hey, babe," he said, but his eyes didn't hold mine. They kept flicking around the room until they stopped. He was handsome, but more so when a sudden smile overtook his face. I tried to look where he was, but I couldn't see whoever he was seeing. "Later." He walked off quickly, and I tried to watch him, to see who he was obviously in love with, but he disappeared into the crowd.

Tipping my head back, I caught Dustin's gaze. "You've been here a few times?"

"Yeah, with Carter back in the day when Court and State first got together. Good group of people. They'd do anything and everything for each other."

"I like that you have people like this in your life."

Dustin's nose brushed over my cheek. "Now they'll be in your life. Court's a bit hard to get rid of."

"I heard that, jerk." Dustin flinched when Court flicked his ear. "Now, stop corrupting my time with Brooke. You can have her later." She passed me my drink and took my other hand. "I have more people she needs to meet."

"But—"

"Nope, she's mine for now." She grinned. "Come on, you have to meet Lucas, who's Saint's brother. They're totally opposite to each other. There's also Wreck, Torch, and Tech."

Leaning back, I quickly lifted up to kiss Dustin on the lips. I wanted him to know I wasn't leaving his side on purpose.

His smile was soft, his eyes warm as he brushed my lips with his. "I'll come find you soon."

"Okay." There was that word again. Courtney tugged on my arm, and I followed along with a laugh. Already I knew my night would be way better than my day, and I couldn't help but feel an excited tingle in my belly over the thought of alone time with Dustin when he drove me home.

Hours later, I stood in the parking area out front of the compound and waved liked a madwoman. "Bye, guys. I love you all. Seriously, you guys are the best. I'm gonna name all my babies after you."

Laughter rang out, but I didn't care because I was so darn happy.

"Bye, bitch," Courtney called, waving just as crazy from State's arms. He'd picked her up bridal style when she nearly face-planted onto the floor since it was moving a lot. We'd both cackled over it for a while.

Dustin chuckled from behind me, with his hands on my waist. I glanced over my shoulder and then faced him when I didn't want to stop looking at him. "Look at you."

"What are you thinkin', darlin'?"

Shaking my head, I curled my arms around his waist. "Court," I yelled. "Look who wanted to date *me*."

"I know, girl, you're so lucky, but not as lucky as me."

I snorted. "Please, mine's better."

"No way, ho. Mine is."

"Dusty, get your drunk outta here before they bitch-slap each other." Humor laced State's deep growly voice.

With my face buried in Dustin's armpit since he smelled delicious, I yelled, "Court, does he use that voice in bed?"

"Oh yeah."

There were groans and more chuckles.

Looking back up to mine, I told him seriously, "I need to bottle your scent."

He snorted. "Is that why your nose is in my armpit?"

"Yes. I could live on it forever, and do you know, even though State's voice is cool, I love yours better." Resting my chin on his chest, I added, "I even played with myself listening to your voice messages."

Dustin's jaw tightened, and I ran a finger over it. Why was his chest moving so fast? "Right. Time to go, darlin'."

"Really?"

His lips twitched. "Yeah, we're already outside near the car."

Blinking slowly, I took in the open space around me. "Hey, we are." Turning, I waved again. "Bye, love you all."

"We love you!" Courtney called.

Dustin swept me up in his arms, and I noticed the passenger door was already open. "Bye." The door closed, but I heard a few responses before it did. I watched Dustin walk around the front and waited for him to climb in, but it seemed to take forever, and my eyes were suddenly so heavy. I had to close them while I waited, just for a little while.

CHAPTER ELEVEN

DUSTIN

A groan of pain woke me the next morning. Wiping the sleep from my eyes, I heard it again, and then there were feet shuffling. Smiling, I sat up from the couch to see Brooke round the corner. Half her hair stuck to her face, makeup smeared across her usually fresh skin, and the jersey she wore looked wrinkled.

"Rough night, buttercup?"

A scream tore through the house as she spun my way, clutching her heart. Her eyes were already round but rounded even more when she spotted me standing from the couch. "Dustin."

"Morning, darlin'." I winked, thinking of my drunk Brooke the previous night. How affectionate she was, how sweet and so damn funny. But, of course, my dick remembered the words she muttered about touching herself when she listened to my voice messages. I'd nearly lost my mind and taken her mouth, but I knew if I had, it would have led to a show for the Diamond MC, and I wasn't willing for anyone to see Brooke naked but me.

"Dustin." She backed up a step.

"That's right."

"You're... here."

"Yes." I grinned.

"Oh my God." She covered her face with her hands and ran for the hallway. Only with her hands over her face, she overshot it and slammed into the wall. I winced as I moved over to her and took her in my arms. I tried to pry her hands away from her face, but she shook her head.

"Are you all right?"

"Yes. Please, go and let me die."

Chuckling, I kissed her forehead and rubbed her back. "Not leaving, darlin'. Why are you all shy now, hmm? You certainly weren't last night."

Her hands went to my tee and gripped. She shook me a little. "That was drunk Brooke. Drunk Brooke is... too much. I'm more myself now."

"I like both sides."

She groaned and dropped her forehead to my chest. I rubbed the back of her neck. "I'm so sorry for drinking so much and ruining our night."

"Brooke, you didn't ruin it. Honestly, I had a blast, and it was great to see you relax and let your hair down. You're a very cute drunk."

"What did I do?"

"You can't remember it?"

She shrugged. "Bits and pieces."

Smiling, I kissed the top of her head. "How about you go shower while I get some food going and we'll talk about it?"

"A shower sounds good."

"All right."

"But it means moving."

Chuckling, I offered, "I could help you in the shower—"

"I'm off." She slipped around me and went back down the hall. Smiling, I walked into the kitchen and had a look to see what I could cook. I already knew she wanted to take things slow from last night when she told me as she got into bed. Even though I was hot as sin—her words, not mine—and she was ready to ride me all night long—yeah, that one drove me crazy—she thought I was special and wanted this to last. That we had to be patient and work each other out because she knew we'd annoy each other at times but staying strong through those arguments was what's important.

A scream chilled me to the bones. I ran down the hall and tried to open the door where I heard Brooke ranting, "No, no, no, no."

"Brooke, what's wrong? Open the door. I can help."

The door swung open, and she pointed at her face. "You saw me like this? I can't take that shit back. Now you know I'm a zombie in the mornings on my good days. Hungover… it's a whole new level." She gestured to her whole body.

Biting my bottom lip to try to contain my grin, I cupped her cheek. "You look cute. Nothing to worry about, darlin'."

Her eyes narrowed. "Are you… okay? Like in the head?"

An abrupt laugh left me and I tugged her into my arms.

"I'm more than okay. There's nothing that could turn me off you."

"You make no sense."

"Why?"

Her head shook against me. "Nothing. I'll go shower." With her head ducked, she turned and shut the door to the bathroom again. "Dustin," she said behind the door.

"Darlin'?"

"Thank you."

"I'm not sure what for, but you're welcome."

"For taking care of me last night and... for accepting me as is."

My chest inflated with how big my heart felt. I pressed my fingers to the door. "I would always accept you, Brooke Baker. I was a fucking fool to begin with, but I see it now. We do have something to work on between us and I look forward to seeing where it goes."

She groaned. "You can't be all cute and sweet when I can't kiss you."

Grinning, I rested my forehead on the door. "You can kiss me, darlin'."

"After, when I'm not breathing morning-breath fire."

Snorting, I tapped two fingers on the door and straightened. "All right."

In the kitchen, I found eggs and bacon and knew it'd be a good hangover fix. Honestly, I was glad I got to see Brooke drunk. It showed me what was on the inside of her. There were mean drunks, idiot drunks, and cute drunks like Brooke, who loved everything and everyone. Though she didn't show everyone the same amount of attention as much as she did me, and hell, it made me like her that much more.

I was sure luck shone down on me the day I got my head out of my ass and actually *saw* Brooke. I still wanted to kick myself for making that mistake in the first place. I wished I'd seen it right from the start.

Brooke was so much more than I'd thought from the first time I'd met her at the bar when she talked about her anal beads. She was kind, caring, and, I'd learned over our phone calls, easy to talk to. I felt I could share so much with her.

Stealing a piece of cooked bacon, I readied the eggs. Hopefully, she wasn't one of the women who took forever in the bathroom or her food would go cold. I quickly placed some bread in the toaster and then stretched since I hadn't had the best of sleep on the couch. Still, it was worth it to see Brooke in the morning. I also stayed to make sure she wasn't sick through the night, and even though she asked and begged a little, I didn't sleep in her bed, knowing she would have got the shock of her life in the morning.

A phone rang. I turned to see Brooke's lighting up on the kitchen table, where she had dropped it the night before. Shifting over after I turned the eggs, I saw Reagan's name on the screen.

Would Brooke mind if I answered? No doubt she would have told Reagan we were dating, right?

Picking it up, I lifted my shoulder and put it to my ear as I went back to cooking. "Hi, Reagan, it's Dustin. Brooke's just in the shower."

Silence.

The toast popped up and I got them out. "Reagan?"

More silence. Finally a noise, kind of like an unsteady breath, followed. A wheeze.

Then I heard Carter's voice in the background. "Ree, what are you doing?" There was a pause and then "Hello?"

"Carter, it's Dustin. I answered Brooke's phone."

Carter started laughing. "That's why my girlfriend has a red, shocked face. Wait… why are you at her house so early? Dustin, what the fuck, man? You can't just stay the night on the first date."

Snorting, I shook my head and plated up the food. "Says the man who moved into his woman's house before they were even together?"

"That was different. It was her parents' idea."

"You just got lucky. But relax, I stayed on the couch. Brooke had a few too many at the compound, so I stayed the night to keep an eye on her."

"Aww, that's so nice," I heard Reagan coo. "Get Brooke to call me when she can."

"Will do, and hey, we should go on a double date soon."

"Yes!" was Reagan's response.

"Looks like we will." Carter chuckled. "Talk soon, yeah?"

"You got it, Coach." I placed Brooke's phone back on the table and went to prepare some coffees. I still couldn't believe Carter wasn't on the team and instead was taking up a coaching position. I knew I had a few years left in me yet before my body had enough, and I still enjoyed football to want to keep going, but after that time, I still didn't have a clue in what I wanted to do. It was something I needed to work out soon.

Hands landed on my waist, and breasts were pressed into my back.

As I turned, Brooke's hand slid with my body and stayed on my hips. "Feeling better?"

"Much." Her hair was damp, her face makeup free, and I saw the splatter of freckles across her nose. She wore some shorts and a tee with a band on it. She looked perfect.

"Good. Breakfast is ready, but I'm going to need that morning kiss now."

Her eyes darkened. "I could do that." As she went to her toes, I dipped, our mouths touching. Another followed before I wrapped my arms around Brooke's shoulders and our grips tightened while we *kissed* each other.

Lightning struck through my system. Kissing Brooke was like a charge to the body, and I never wanted it to end. Only there were things we still needed. Like oxygen.

With a heavy breath, I rested my forehead to Brooke's. A small laugh escaped her. "I could get used to kisses like that."

"I know the feeling." Straightening, I smiled down at her. "Let's eat."

She nodded and moved over to the table. I quickly finished the coffees and brought hers over. "Thank you again for staying. Though, you didn't have to."

"I know. I wanted to." We ate in silence for a little while and I settled into the comfort of it. I didn't feel the need to fill it with random shit. I liked watching her. I liked eating with her and smiling when our eyes connected.

Christ, I was lost in her.

Brooke managed to eat over half before she pushed her

plate away and picked up her coffee. "It was lovely, but I'm stuffed. Must have been all the drinking last night."

Smirking, I nodded as I took a sip of my coffee. "Did I get your coffee right?"

"You did. How did you remember?"

"At Nana Bev's when she complained how you have no sugar in it, but at least you have cream."

"You remember that?"

"I do. I also remember you telling me last night that you touch yourself when you listen to my voice messages."

Coffee sprayed the table from her mouth. Her eyes rounded, and I worried they'd pop out of her head. "I did not."

Grinning, I leaned into the table. "You did."

Brooke covered her eyes with her hand. "Dear God, what else did I say?" She removed her hand to wave it in front of her. "Actually, no, don't tell me. I don't want to know."

"Are you sure?"

"Yes. No. Yes. I mean… at least you didn't run away after it. That's good, isn't it?"

"It is." I smiled.

Suddenly she paled.

"Did you remember something?"

Brooke winced. "Did I…" She blew out a breath. "Did I keep sniffing you?"

Chuckling, I nodded. "Yep."

She groaned. "And you're still here."

"How could I be offended by you liking the way I smell? It also didn't bother me when you told me I'd be the lucky one where you'd hump my leg." She groaned again and covered her face. "Or, when you and Courtney got into an argument over who had the better eye color between State and me." She shook her head. "You may have tried to adopt Lucas, Saint's brother. However, Wreck, his partner, wouldn't let you."

"Please, no more."

"But my favorite was when you told me that one day you were going to marry me."

Her head lifted with eyes wide as she gasped. "I did not."

My lips twitched. She had. She also mentioned how she couldn't wait to have sex with me, but I wasn't going to bring that up.

"I am so, so sorry."

"There's nothing to forgive. I had an amazing night."

She shook her head. "Come on, that was terrible for a first date. I'll never drink again."

"Our first date was at Nana Bev's, and you will drink again, since you promised the others at the compound that you'll be back for the next family night."

"I can't face them. I tried to braid Death's hair."

Thinking of it had me laughing. "You stopped when I got close."

Another groan dropped from her lips before she slumped in her seat and hit her head to the table. "I did because I said you were like my new favorite toy that I wanted to play with all the time."

Grinning, I reached out and patted her arm. "I've never been happier to be called a toy." Seriously, she had nothing to worry about from the night before. Everything she did or said made me like her that much more. I hadn't laughed as much as I had last night. "Honestly, darlin', don't worry about it. I had a great night."

She lifted her head enough to peek up at me. "You did?"

"I did."

"I promise the next time will be better."

"Any time with you is good, darlin'. In time you'll understand that I don't care what we do, where we go, as long as I get to spend time with you."

Her eyes softened. She quickly stood, and I shifted back when she came at me. Within seconds, I had her sitting on my lap, facing me. Her hands cupped the back of my neck and mine went to her waist, even though they itched to grip her ass.

"You can't say sweet things to me and not expect me to react."

"I'm liking the way you react, darlin'."

She leaned in, and against my ear she whispered, "I'm glad you do." She took my earlobe between her lips and sucked on it.

My cock shot straight to hard, as if it thought it was getting sucked on. My hand tightened on her waist before I wrapped my arms around her and brought her close.

"Fuck, Brooke." I groaned when she licked the edge of my ear. Slamming my eyes closed, I fought the idea of having her ride me in this position. I struggled against slipping my hands down the back of her shorts and cupping her ass. The way she licked, sucked, and nipped at my ear felt like it was pulling strings right to my dick. It throbbed, jerked, and I wanted to slide into her heat so bad.

You're so special. We need to take it slow because I want this to last.

Her words from the night before rang through my mind.

If this didn't stop, there would be no slow about it. Opening my eyes, I stood and helped her slowly slide her feet to the floor. She was shocked by the abrupt movement, her eyes wide and worried. When she brushed over my erection, her eyes shifted to understanding and warmth.

Stepping back, I gripped my dick behind my jeans and adjusted. "Sorry, didn't know my ear was that sensitive."

She laughed, and a blush hit her cheeks. "Never apologize for *that* reaction. If I was a guy, I'd have a boner right now." She took our plates from the table and went to the sink.

Walking up behind her, I wrapped my arms around her waist, not so close that I pressed my dick into her, and asked, "Did you have plans for the day?"

"I didn't." She scraped off the leftovers into the garbage disposal and rinsed the plates. "Do you want to watch a movie or something? I'm sorry, I don't think I'm up for too much."

"A movie sounds good." Dipping down, I kissed her neck and shifted to the dishwasher. I loaded the plates and glanced to see Brooke watching me. I cocked a brow. "What?"

"I just never thought I'd see a guy who's so domesticated."

"When it came to being a dad, I had to learn quick. Though, I'll admit I do have a cleaner come in every second week."

"I knew you couldn't be *that* good. To cook, work out, play football, travel, take care of Benjie, *and* clean." She shook her head. "Now I know you're not that perfect, I don't think we can date, sorry."

She tried to move by me, but I spun her into my arms so her back was to my front, and at her ear, I told her, "You forgot one. I'm a master in bed also."

"Sure," she drew out, but I caught her shiver.

"You'll see, eventually."

"I think I remember saying we should go slow. You know I'm also a liar when drunk?"

Laughing, I shook my head and dropped my hands, but couldn't resist a light tap to her gorgeous ass as I walked by her. "That I don't believe."

"Really, ask anyone."

"No."

I heard her following. "I'm serious, Dustin. I'm the biggest liar out there when I'm drunk."

Sitting on the couch, I chuckled at her antics. "You can't have your way with me, woman."

"But—"

"No. Now get over here and sit down. I'll let you cuddle me, but that's about it."

"So, no handsies?"

Choking, I shook my head and threw a cushion at her. "Yes. Wait, no! No hand jobs."

"What about light groping?"

The thought of her with her hands on me had me groaning. "No. I'm a born-again virgin. Treat me as such."

A giggle escaped her. She sat next to me on the couch, her lips twitching. "Is sitting close okay?"

"I'll allow it." I threw my arm around her shoulders.

"Whoa, isn't that too much for a born-again virgin?"

"Shut it, smartass." My dick was still half-hard and stuck on the image of a hand job. Even though I enjoyed the banter, I was serious about taking it slow, and I knew she was as well. Especially when a future together was at stake.

CHAPTER TWELVE

BROOKE

For the life of me I couldn't remember why I'd suggested going slow. All right, that was a lie. I did. I wanted what Dustin and I were exploring to last. I thought taking it slow would help and he wouldn't get bored with me. But I didn't realize how much restraint the man had and how much I wanted him to throw caution to the wind and fuck me. In the bed, on the floor, or the counter, even in the car would do.

"Miss Brooke" was yelled across the restaurant before I saw Benjie running toward me with his arms out. My heart melted right there to see such joy on the child's face, and it was all for me.

"Benjie." I swept him up in my arms and hugged him close.

I hadn't seen him since I'd taken him to pick Dustin up from the airport. I'd missed the little guy.

I'd seen his father though. Dustin and I had seen each other three times in the last two weeks. Once was at his place, another out to dinner, the last was when he dropped into dinner with Nana Bev again. Other than that, his schedule was busy, and I knew he headed away on Monday. He'd be gone a whole week for some promotional events the team had to do. It was why he'd got Benjie early from Emily.

"How have you been?"

"Good. What are you going to get to eat? I was thinking the pasta, but then Dad pointed out the chicken nuggets, and I love them."

"How about I get some pasta and you can have some of mine?"

His gaze grew. "You would do that?"

"Of course." I placed him on his feet and took his hand.

He hugged my hand with both of his. "Thank you."

Smiling down at him, I winked. "You're welcome." Glancing to the table, my smile widened when I saw Dustin watching us. He wasn't the only one. Carter and Reagan were here also, but they knew not to say anything to Benjie about Dustin and me. We had to pretend to be friends and that was all. I could do it, even when all I wanted to do was lean down and kiss Dustin hello.

"Hi, everyone."

Benjie took the seat next to his dad and I sat beside him, opposite Reagan. I would have liked to sit next to Dustin and sneak some hand-holding in, but I couldn't complain. I was just happy to be there with them all. Heck, I'd been the happiest I had in a long time since I'd let down my walls and started dating Dustin.

It made me wonder why I'd been so adamant about nothing happening between us in the first place. But glancing down at Benjie, I knew there was still some worry there.

"Brooke, good to see you." Dustin winked over Benjie's head.

"You also." I grinned.

"Carter, how's life as a coach?" I asked. I'd seen Reagan at work today, so I knew how she was doing.

"I can say my body is happy I'm out of the grueling workouts two times a day."

Dustin rolled his eyes. "Yeah, yeah, we can't all be couch potatoes."

Carter grinned, leaned back, and curled an arm around Reagan's shoulders. "What's been happening with you t— fuck." Carter cringed as he pushed his chair back and, no doubt, rubbed his shin. I didn't think I was the only one who'd kicked him either.

Benjie straightened quickly and pointed at Carter. "Bad word. You have to put a dollar in the jar." Carter nodded, still rubbing at his leg. I'd thought he was going to ignore Carter's question, until he added, "What does Carter mean? Is there something happening?" Benjie asked, looking from Dustin to me and back again.

Ruffling his hair, I told him, "He was just asking us what we've both been up to lately."

"Oh." His shoulders rounded, seeming a little deflated. It was another reason we couldn't say anything until Dustin and I were sure we were it for each other. We hadn't even had an argument yet, since it was early days still, so I didn't know if he was an unreasonable dick who would just piss me off each time. "Can I go play on the playground for a little bit?"

"How about I come with?" I offered before Dustin could say anything.

"I'm okay on my own. It's just over there and locked up like a jail."

That was true, yet there could be bullies in there, and I didn't want Benjie to not have backup.

Thinning my lips, I said, "I'm not sure."

Dustin's fingers brushed against my arm along the back of Benjie's chair. "He'll be fine. He knows if there's any trouble to shout out or come back."

Nodding, I helped Benjie scoot his chair back. "Be safe, and don't climb on anything too high."

Benjie just gave me a look and laughed. "It's not my first playground. You took me to that one near your house. Can we go again sometime soon?"

"Heck yes."

"And maybe this time a stranger won't ask you for your number."

"What's this now?" Dustin asked.

Benjie shrugged. "It was just some man." He skipped off to the indoor playground.

Carter chuckled. "I think that kid's a genius."

Reagan shushed him and was no doubt looking at me and Dustin, who hadn't moved his gaze from me.

"Didn't we talk about this?" I asked him.

"No, I would have remembered."

I threw up a hand. "It was the first time I met Benjie. Some guy at the playground approached and was talking to me. Honestly, I can't remember much of it. But I do remember Benjie coming over and yelling stranger danger. It got rid of the guy pretty quick."

"Was this before or after you changed from that hot little black dress?"

"Oh, now you want to note that dress? Yet you took someone else…. Forget it because it was a long time ago."

"Benjie really yelled stranger danger?" Dustin asked, and I was glad he dropped what I'd been about to bring up because I didn't want to live in the past. Our time was about our future.

I smiled. "He did."

Dustin glanced at Carter. "You're right, my son is a genius."

"When do you think you'll tell him?" Reagan asked.

"Not sure, right?" I asked Dustin.

"Yeah, we'll go with the flow, and when we feel it's right, we'll do it." His eyes warmed. "Wish I could have kissed you hello though."

"I thought the same thing."

"Awww." We glared at Carter.

While the guys spoke about the game, Reagan leaned closer and I did the same. "Can I just say how cute it is to see you and Benjie together?"

My heart thumped. "He's an amazing kid."

"He thinks you're amazing as well. Anyone can see it. Before you arrived, it was all about looking for you, waiting for you to walk through the door. I can under-stand why you're not saying anything to him yet. I think he's already in love with the idea of his dad being with you."

"That's what I was thinking too."

"Still, I'm glad you're giving this a chance. Benjie's face wasn't the only one that lit up when you arrived. Dustin's happy, and I can tell you are also. It's great to see."

"Right back at you."

She smiled and glanced at Carter. Her eyes softened before she looked back to me. "Yeah, he makes me happy." Reagan leaned back. "Did you tell Dustin that Tom found out about you and him?"

"Tom who I met at Reagan's and is your boss?" Dustin asked.

"That would be the one." Reagan smirked.

It had completely slipped my mind when I arrived, but I had to warn him because—

"Sorry I'm late."

Damn it.

"Ah, Tom wanted to join us for dinner," I said and shrugged apologetically.

"Tom, you'll need to sit around here." Reagan tapped the table and got Carter to inch down closer to her so Tom would be directly across from Dustin.

"Actually, we'll need to join another table. I have a couple of people coming." He grinned before he got a waiter's attention and asked for just that.

"Tom, what did you do?" I asked.

"Me?" He moved around the table to sit where Reagan directed him to. "Nothing. I just happened to drop into a friend's house after work to brag—"

"You didn't!" Reagan clipped and even went as far as reaching across the table to grab him. She probably would have shaken him if Carter hadn't reached out to stop her with a chuckle.

"What did he do?" Dustin asked. Humor lit his eyes. "Good to see you again, Tom," he added.

Tom slowly looked at Dustin and raised a brow as he leaned back in his seat. If he was trying to look intimidating, it wasn't working. "Is it?"

Dustin's lips twitched. "Well, I thought it was. Have I done something?"

Tom nodded once at Dustin. "You tell me?"

What in the world was he doing? He'd seemed excited when he invited himself to dinner.

"Tom—"

"Hello, hi, over here."

Reagan groaned and slapped her forehead. I knew that voice anywhere. Reagan's parents were on their way over, and just in time was the waiter with the extra table.

Dear God. I slid down in my seat a little.

"Isn't this lovely?" Elaine beamed at us from down the table. She took the seat beside Dustin. "When Tom mentioned he was having dinner with you all, I just had to come along. She looked down the table and waved to Reagan. "Hello, honey."

"Hey." It sounded a little hesitant.

"Herb, Elaine, great to see you both," Carter greeted.

"Son." Herb nodded. "I can call you son, right? I mean, you're dating my daughter. It's not too early for it?" He probably hadn't realized he'd been calling Carter son for some time now.

Carter chuckled. "I'm fine with it."

Dustin caught my gaze. His smile told me he was loving this. He didn't know what he was in for since he'd only been around them all together the once and we'd been busy moving Carter into Reagan's that day.

"Herb, Elaine, it's great to see you both." Dustin held his hand out for Herb to shake.

Herb looked down at it and then over to Tom. "Have you started?"

"Not yet."

"Good." He sat down, and both Tom and Herb stared Dustin down. I was somewhat scared for him. Especially since I knew nothing about what was going on.

"Right," Tom started.

"We need to give you a piece of advice," Herb put in.

Tom nodded. "Brooke has been in our lives a long time—"

"Tom, Herb, you don't need to say—"

Tom's hand shot up my way. "As I was saying, she's been in our lives a long time, so we want you to know that even though you play for the Wolves, if you hurt her, we'll bring a world of pain your way."

"World of pain," Herb added, nodding.

Gaping at them, a part of me wanted to give them a hug. Another part wanted to tell them I was old enough to take care of myself. I glanced at Reagan to see her hand over her face, shaking her head, while her mother nodded along with her husband as she stared at Dustin. Carter chuckled, and

Dustin looked back at them with a serious face as he rested his elbows to the table and linked his fingers together.

"I understand, and I need you both to know I have acknowledged I was stupid at the start, but I've learned my lesson, and Brooke will always be one of the most important people in my life."

Oh shit.

Swoon.

My belly and heart danced together.

Tom and Herb shared a look. Tom grinned at Dustin. "Okay then."

Herb couldn't be left out though. "But it doesn't mean we won't be watching you."

Dustin nodded. "I completely understand."

"Good. Elaine." Herb held his hand out to his wife, and she pulled her bag to the table and pulled out a jersey and handed it over to Herb, who then passed it to Dustin. "Can I get you to sign this?"

Dustin laughed. "Of course." He took the jersey and offered Sharpie and signed his name across the back where I saw Carter's name.

It was then I saw Benjie running up toward the table. "Tom, Herb, and Elaine. Benjie doesn't know about us, so please don't say anything."

"Our lips are sealed." Elaine winked.

When Benjie arrived, Dustin introduced him to the others since they hadn't met. Elaine pressed her hands to her cheeks. "My, aren't you a mini Dustin. Such a handsome boy."

Benjie smiled at her before he turned to me. "Miss Brooke, do you think Daddy's handsome?"

Everyone froze at the table.

"I… ah… well, sure, buddy."

"He thinks you're pretty. I heard him telling Mr. North about it."

Biting my bottom lip, I controlled my laughter with a cough. "That's nice."

Thankfully, a waiter arrived and took our orders, and by the time he left, Benjie had forgotten what he'd been talking about. Dustin was going to have to be very careful when he spoke on the phone to me or with someone about me. If not, little fox ears would hear it.

"Speaking of North, do you know what's up with him lately?" Carter asked Dustin.

Dustin shook his head. "Nope, but he's been ignoring my calls and texts."

"We'll have to pay him a visit."

"Maybe we could go after dinner?" Reagan suggested.

Elaine clapped. "Oh, I know, would you mind if Herb and I took Benjie for ice cream, and we could meet back at Reagan's for you to pick him up?"

"What do you think, Benjie?" his dad asked.

"I could go with you if you're not comfortable around people you've just met." I rested my hand on Benjie's shoulder. I'd been lucky he'd somehow trusted me that first time, but I didn't want him to think he had to go with them alone if he wasn't comfortable.

"No, it's okay." Benjie smiled. "You can go with Daddy in his car and come pick me up after seeing Mr. North."

He was pushing me toward his father more and more. My belly warmed, convinced he'd accepted me to be important in his life, so much so, he wanted me with his dad. But there was also that niggling feeling in the pit of my stomach that worried about things not working out. Only, for the first time, I shoved that worry down because I wanted this to work.

"Sounds like a plan, kiddo." Dustin ruffled his hair. He glanced to Carter. "We'll follow you."

"Got it." Carter grinned as he cupped the back of Reagan's neck and massaged his fingers into it.

There wasn't a time limit on how slow to take things between Dustin and me, but I couldn't help but want to show the public affection Carter showed Reagan, but with Dustin and me. Still, I could wait. I had a feeling it would be worth it in the end.

CHAPTER THIRTEEN

DUSTIN

*I*t was good to hold Brooke's hand on the drive to North's. Bringing it to my lips, I kissed her knuckles and she rewarded me with a warm smile.

"I have a feeling your son wants us to date."

Chuckling, I nodded and rested our hands on her thigh. "I agree. He's never been like this. Then again, he hasn't met anyone else... besides Letta that day." I winced, bringing it up.

All Brooke did was squeeze my hand. "It's because I won him over with ice cream and a playground."

"I doubt it. It's your charm and sweet nature."

"Oh, I'm not sweet. Just as my work colleagues would say."

"You do remember Reagan is one."

She rolled her eyes. "Reagan is biased because we've known each other for a long time."

I snorted. "I doubt that." Speaking of her work reminded me of a student she'd been talking about. One night when I called, she'd sounded upset. She didn't really want to share, but I got it out of her eventually. "How did it go with your student?"

"Better. I finally got him to understand it needed to be reported or, at the very least, if he wanted me to speak to his mom since he wasn't sure she knew it was going on when she wasn't there. After I reported it to Tom, and we contacted the police, we all went together to his mother, since the student wanted support from me and Tom. As the kid had thought, his mom had no idea. Then we all waited until the father got home and the wife kicked him out and placed a restraining order on him."

"He's lucky he has a mother who would protect their child over anything."

"That's exactly what I thought. It makes me sad when I think of the kids who don't have anyone and go through that type of situation without reaching out for help."

"You're a strong woman to have the type of job you have."

She shrugged. "I have support when I need it."

Lifting her hand, I brushed my lips against it again. "You do, and now you have more. I'll always be here when you need to get things off your chest."

She smiled over at me, her gaze soft. "There you go again, saying sweet stuff when I can't reward you for it with a kiss."

My gut tingled. "Lucky we're here then." I pulled to a stop out front of North's townhouse. Switching off the car, I unhooked my seat belt and then Brooke's before I cupped the back of her head and tugged her close. I caught her big smile and felt it against my lips until I nipped at her bottom lip. She then brought her tongue out to play with mine.

The kiss shot straight from mild to hot in seconds. One of Brooke's hands landed on my shoulder, the other slid up and down my thigh. Of course, my dick noticed and hardened, ready for her hand's attention.

A knock sounded on the window. We both jumped apart, breathing heavily.

"Fuck." I scrubbed a hand down my face and sent the middle finger to Carter, who was grinning through the window.

"Come on. I'm freezing my balls off out here." He rubbed his hands together as he moved over to Reagan and wrapped his arms around her.

Turning back to Brooke, I dipped in for another quick kiss. "Come back to my place for a little while after we get Benjie?"

She bit her bottom lip, then licked them. "I don't know."

"Darlin', I need more time with you before I leave. I'll make sure you get home in a taxi. I'll even pay."

She laughed. "It's not that. What happens if Benjie sees something he shouldn't?"

"We'll get him to bed first before anything."

"All right."

My grin was wide. "Good, come on then. Let's go see what's up North's ass." I took the keys and climbed out, waiting for Brooke. Hand in hand, we followed Carter and Reagan up to the front door on the porch.

Carter knocked and we waited. Then waited some more. I

reached through the space between Carter and Reagan and knocked louder. We heard footsteps, but then nothing for a little while. Carter and I shared a look, both wondering what was going on.

Carter rapped on the door again, more footsteps sounded inside, and finally the door opened a little.

"What?" North clipped.

"We thought we'd drop by to see how our friend is," Carter answered.

"Yeah, the friend who won't take our calls or texts," I added.

North sighed. "Look, now's not a good time—" Something smashed inside the house, and someone cursed. He had someone in there. He'd never said he was into someone.

What was going on?

North looked behind him. "Shit. Hang on." He left the door and stalked down the hallway.

"The door's open," I stated the obvious.

"We can't." Reagan gripped Carter's arm.

"But someone could be hurt," Brooke said with a shrug. I was glad my woman was on the side of invading personal spaces when worried about a friend.

"Look out." With Brooke's hand in mine, I slipped through Carter and Reagan and pushed the door open more to walk in. Quietly, we went down the hall and two voices grew louder the closer we got to the kitchen.

Until they stopped and something else was knocked over.

Stepping around the corner, I froze while Brooke made a noise in the back of her throat.

LILA ROSE

Carter and Reagan ran into us. Carter cursed, then choked, and Reagan sucked in a breath.

The two people across from us jumped apart. North ran a hand over his head of black hair. "Fucking hell. Do you usually just walk into anyone's house?"

Lifting a hand, I pointed from North to the other person. "You and you."

Brooke patted my arm. "Good boy, using your words." She turned back to North. "Sorry, North, but these two knuckleheads have been worried about you, so we thought to drop in." She smiled to the other person. "Hi, I'm Brooke. I'm dating Dustin, who's on the Wolves with North. That's Carter and Reagan."

"We know him," I managed to get out.

"Wait." Carter ran a hand over his face. "When did this happen? Are you two dating?"

The man who Carter and I knew, and who was glaring at all of us, shook his head. "We're not dating."

North's body jolted before he turned to him. "We're not?"

Brooke nudged my side with her elbow. "Who is he?"

"I'm out." The guy started to move around North and head for the hallway toward the front door.

"You might want more clothes on," I suggested.

He cursed and turned, heading for the main bedroom.

"Excuse me a minute," North said, following him.

As soon as North had gone, Brooke turned to me. "Who is he?"

"His name's Jack Jennings. He's an asshole who we never got along with, but also on the team."

"Oh. Well, that's awkward."

Reagan nodded. "We should leave them to it."

Yeah, it definitely looked like they had shit to sort through. We shuffled back into the hallway, and I called, "North, we're hitting the road, but next time don't ignore our calls or texts."

"Later" was the only response we got.

Brooke shoved her elbow into my ribs again. "Say goodbye to Jack."

"What? Why? He doesn't like me."

"So?"

"You do it, Carter." Reagan shoved at her man a little.

"Hell no."

Brooke threw a hand up. "Now it's just going to be strange no one had said goodbye to him. It's not like we didn't see him in there kissing North like he was a starved man."

Reagan giggled. "You saw that too."

Brooke fanned herself. "Boy, did I ever."

"Hey, don't go getting any ideas. I'm not kissing a guy for you."

"Me neither," Carter added.

Brooke rolled her eyes. "Bye, North and Jack Jennings," she yelled.

Silence.

"Yeah, bye."

My eyes widened when it was Jennings's rough voice that called out. At least he was being polite for the first time, and I wouldn't have to kick his ass for ignoring Brooke. Because I would. The guy had a few pounds on me, but I could take him and his dark attitude.

Once outside, we congregated near the cars. I broke the ice first by asking Carter, "Did you know North was gay?"

He shook his head. "Didn't have a clue since the only dates I'd ever seen with him were women."

I wound my arm around Brooke's shoulders when she curled an arm around my waist, saying, "He could be bisexual and wasn't sure coming out was a good idea."

"But we're his friends." It actually stung he hadn't thought he could tell Carter and me at least that he was into guys. Not that he had to, but it wasn't like we'd care. We'd never said anything bad about same-sex relationships. Each to their own as long as they were happy.

"We'll have to talk to him," Carter said, lips thinning, probably feeling that same sting. Reagan wrapped her arms around his waist.

My eyes bulged. "I'm going away with them. Do I pretend it never happened? Do I talk to North then or wait for him to come to me? I don't know what to do." Leaning in, I whispered, "Am I supposed to make friends with Jennings? He's in North's life and North is our buddy."

Carter snorted. "I'm glad it's you and not me."

Looking to Brooke, since she was wiser than me, I asked, "What do I do?"

She smiled. "Just be there for him when he does come to you. Don't pressure him into answers, but if you get a chance of being alone while away, talk to him. If he doesn't want to answer, leave it. He'll come around."

"If he hasn't said anything when away, we'll get together with him for a guys' night," Carter suggested. "But we won't pressure him then either. If he wants to talk, he can."

"All right, I can do this. But what about Jennings?"

Reagan winced. "I wouldn't approach him or talk to him about North unless he comes to you first."

"You two have never got along with him?" Brooke asked.

Carter answered, "He's never gotten along with anyone. His walls are tall and thick. It's lucky he's a good team player on the field. Off, he's always stuck to himself."

I shrugged. "Not that we haven't tried. After a year of asking him to grab a drink or dinner and getting declined, we gave in and let him be. We don't hate the guy, we just don't know him. All right, maybe we got a bit annoyed he'd never made an effort to get to know us when we'd tried."

Brooke's lips thinned. Carter, North, and I had always presumed something terrible must have happened in Jennings's life for him to be this way, but it wasn't like he'd tell us, and it was another reason we'd let him be since it was clear he didn't want any help, and we couldn't force ourselves on him. I couldn't believe I hadn't noticed North and Jennings getting closer. Unless they'd hidden it like their relationship... or whatever it would be in the end.

Brooke shifted on her feet. "We'd better get moving in case Jennings busts out that door. Plus, we need to save Benjie from his sugar coma that no doubt Elaine has put him in."

Reagan grinned. "That's true."

Carter nodded. "We'll meet you there."

In the car, Brooke turned to me as I started the engine. "Are you okay?"

Thinning my lips, I nodded.

"Dustin" was all she said, and it had me spilling those gross emotions.

"I'm a little gutted North didn't think he could share that side of his life with us."

"I understand you may be hurt, but North coming out has nothing to do with you or anyone else. Though, you know, it could be new to even North. Maybe him and Jennings's hookup was a surprise to North as much as it was for you and Carter?"

Dipping my brows, I pulled the car onto the road. "Is that possible?"

"Heck yes. I've known a few people who didn't realize or accept their sexuality until they were older. It could be one incident or one person that piques their curiosity. But even if North had known longer, that wouldn't change you being friends with him, right?"

"Fuck no."

Her hand cupped my thigh, and my dick said hello. "It'll work out."

"Yeah, it will."

"Would you give Jennings a chance if he stays in North's life?"

"Of course. Whatever makes North happy, I'll deal with it. I'm not too hard to get along with."

She laughed. "No, you're not. Even after a few times of being around you, I decided to like you."

"That was the wrong move."

She smirked. "Oh, why?"

"Because now you're going to be stuck with me."

Her hand tightened on my thigh, and my dick was ready to sing for her. "I don't mind it, *yet*. But I'll let you know if I change my mind."

Shaking my head, I sighed. "I forgot to say there's no take backs. It's not try before you buy. As soon as we kissed, the deal was sealed. It's in the contract."

"Contract?"

"Yes."

She snorted. "And where is this contract? I don't think I've signed anything lately."

"Okay, Nana Bev may have forged your signature, but it looks like the real deal if anyone asks."

Her laughter was long and loud. "Oh God, do not give Nana the idea of signing me over to you. She probably would."

Chuckling, I nodded. "I could actually see her doing it. As long as I promised her great-grandchildren."

Brooke sobered. "Um, do you want more kids?"

Resting my hand over hers, I gave it a squeeze. "Eventually, I'd like a brother or a sister for Benjie."

"Okay."

I brought her hand up and kissed the back of it. "Okay. Something else you should know for when I get back or even weeks after it... I had my blood done and I'm negative."

Brooke coughed, sputtered, and choked. "Holy shit, you're just going to throw that out there."

Grinning, I shrugged. "It's best to get that out of the way."

"All right then." She nodded. "You should know since I had to check my iron levels, I also got a full blood test done. I'm in the clear, and I'm also on birth control."

Groaning, I realized my mistake. "Maybe it wasn't the best idea talking about it now." Especially since my cock shot from half hard to all the way since he was ready to sink into Brooke bare.

Brooke laughed. "You think? I'm already wishing your time away was over."

"So am I." And usually I didn't, because I breathed football. It showed me how much Brooke had started meaning to me.

CHAPTER FOURTEEN

BROOKE

*a*nd then Mr. Herb and Mr. Tom got into an argument in the ice cream shop about which flavor is the best." Benjie was definitely on a high as we drove back to Dustin's.

"Who won?" Dustin asked, and I didn't miss his gaze or the smirk when he saw I had stuck my hands under my butt so I didn't accidentally reach over and touch him.

"No one. Mrs. Elaine broke them up." He sounded a little annoyed over the matter. Had he hoped for a bloodbath?

Smiling, I turned around in my seat to face him. "What flavor did you get?"

"Chocolate with cookie dough in it. What's another one of your favorites, Miss Brooke? Besides caramel."

"Hmm." I tapped my chin. "I think I like strawberry with sherbet in it."

His grin was blinding. "Daddy likes that too."

I glanced to Dustin. "Do you?"

"I sure do."

"Miss Brooke." Benjie suddenly sounded serious. "Do you like anchovies?"

"What happens if I say I do?"

"Hmm." He tapped his chin. God, he was adorable. "I might have to rethink this friendship."

Both Dustin and I cackled. "Good news then, buddy. I don't."

"Daddy eats them." His nose screwed up.

Dustin smirked. "Nothing wrong with a little fish."

My face burned because my mind took me straight to Dustin between my legs.

"Are you all right there, Brooke?" Dustin smirked.

"Yep, I'm fine."

"Miss Brooke, since you're coming back to our place, can we build that fort?"

"Buddy, it'll be your bedtime when we get home." I caught Dustin wince when he looked into the rearview mirror. I looked there again and saw Benjie's bottom lip tremble. "Brace," Dustin whispered right before Benjie started crying. And I meant *crying*. There were tears and snot everywhere.

"Benjie, you're already tired. You need some sleep," Dustin tried, but the tears wouldn't let up, and he hit the seat a couple of times.

Biting my bottom lip, I reached out and placed a hand on Benjie's knee. "Hey, kiddo. How about I come pick you up one day from your mom's when your dad's away and we can build a fort then?"

He slowed down a little but still gasped slightly. He wiped his eyes. "Really?" He sniffed.

"Yeah, as long as it's okay with your mom and dad."

"O-Okay."

Dustin pulled into the driveway and parked. He got out and collected Benjie while I climbed out and met them at the front. If his outburst wasn't enough, Benjie was exhausted, even wanting to stay in Dustin's arms to be carried inside.

"Miss Brooke." Benjie looked over Dustin's shoulder as we walked down the hallway. "Will you read me a book?"

"I'd love to."

Even his smile was tired.

While Dustin got Benjie ready for bed, I stayed in the living room and turned on the television. Sitting on the couch, I waited until Benjie was ready. It didn't take long before he'd brushed his teeth and was in his pajamas.

Dustin walked into the living room and kissed my forehead. "He's in bed waiting for you. Sorry about in the car. It happens sometimes when he's really tired."

"And probably when he's had a bit of sugar." I stood and got a quick hug off Dustin. "It's bound to happen every now and then. He can't be amazing all the time."

Dustin chuckled. "That's true, just like me."

I snorted. "If you throw a tantrum at your age, it makes me kind of worried."

He smirked. "I'll only do it for a good reason."

Huffing out a laugh, I moved through the house to Benjie's

bedroom. He smiled as soon as I entered, looking cute all tucked into his bed.

"What book would you like to hear?"

"You pick."

I did and shifted over to the bed and sat on the edge beside Benjie. He rested his head on my upper arm and curled his hands around my arm. By the time I was done with the book, he was slouched against the headboard. Slowly, I stood and returned the book before I went back over to the bed and adjusted Benjie so he lay down. Bending, I kissed his forehead, which made him grumble in his sleep and had me smiling.

Making my way back out into the living room, I found Dustin sitting on the couch. I could get used to this and would do everything in my power to make sure I got to keep what I had with Dustin and Benjie.

They were their own little family, even with Emily in it, and I wanted to be a part of it as well. I really did. Dustin made me happy.

Slipping around the couch, he grinned up at me and lifted his arm. I sank to the couch in the crook of his arm.

"Sound asleep?"

With my head on his shoulder, I glanced up. "He is."

His arm tightened around me. "Good."

"What are we watching?" Not that I really wanted to watch a movie since Dustin would be leaving soon and I wanted to spend all the time I could getting to know him. Yet, there was also something else I wanted to do for him before he left. Something he would remember me for. Something I had been thinking about all night.

He kissed my forehead. "Anything you want."

"Anything?"

He shifted to get a better look at my face. "What's those glittery eyes about?"

Straightening, I placed a hand on Dustin's thigh. "What happens if I'm not in the mood to watch a movie?"

He swallowed and cleared his throat. "What did you have in mind?"

I smirked. "A kiss." *To start with.*

He grinned. "I can do that." He reached for me and tugged me close. I placed a hand on his shoulder so I didn't knock heads with him. My other hand remained on his thigh. Our lips touched, caressed, and teased. Dustin slid a hand to my waist and ran it up and down. Only when it went back up, he glided his thumb under my breast.

More was all I could think as our kiss turned up to a different intensity. I scooted closer, my arm hooking around his neck, and I opened my mouth to him, our tongues dancing around one another.

My blood heated, my stomach tumbled, and my heart craved. I needed more. I needed to show him how happy he made me. I wanted to pleasure him.

With a slow hand, I moved the one I'd placed on his thigh up and rubbed over the big bulge in his jeans. Dustin's grip tightened. He cursed against my lips and cupped my breast.

Our kiss went on and on. I didn't need to breathe, because I had more of a need for the man in front of me.

Dustin's hand and fingers pressed and caressed my breast, driving me crazy. His hips lifted into my hand while I rubbed

LILA ROSE

it over him. I slid my finger up and undid the button, then the zip.

Dustin stilled as he broke the kiss. "Darlin'." His tone was gruff and held more of a Southern twang. "We don't have to do anything."

Smiling, I shrugged. "I know." Reaching in his jeans, I pulled out his hard cock and glanced down to see the bead of precum on the tip.

Dustin pressed his thumb under my chin and tipped my head so our gazes locked. "Brooke, don't feel you have to do anything. We can wait until I get back. Then I won't embarrass myself for coming so quick with... fuck." His eyes closed for a moment. "Your hand working me." My hand ran up and down, sliding along his smooth skin.

It was cute how he thought he was only getting my hand.

His jaw clenched, his hips jutting up, and his hand went back to my breast, until I brushed it aside and swept down to take his cock in my mouth.

"Ah, fuck."

Sucking him down to the base, I slowly ran my lips and tongue up and around his thick erection. I slid my mouth back down onto him until the tip hit the back of my throat, and I gagged a little but swallowed around him.

"Jesus Christ, darlin'. This ain't fair." His hand threaded through my hair and tightened, but he didn't use it to force my head. He allowed me to go at the pace I wanted, and I enjoyed the slow torture. I liked the way his body shuddered, the way he moaned and groaned, but especially when he talked. "Darlin', fuck, it feels good. Too good. Christ, I'm seeing stars, Brooke."

I nearly laughed at that one, but when he sucked in a sharp breath, I doubled down my effort for that gold star at the end where I could drink him down.

"Shit, darlin'. I'm close."

His hand moved from my hair and rubbed at my shoulder and back.

"Sweetheart," he groaned, and I looked up from lapping at his tip to see he had his head dropped back. The veins in his neck popped, his body taut. I got down to business and tightened my lips around his dick, sucking up and down over and over while gliding my tongue around every inch of skin I could.

"Brooke." His rough, hard voice was the warning I needed before he came down the back of my throat, and I swallowed it all.

It was then we tensed.

It was then we heard little footsteps.

"Shit, shit, shit. Pretend to be asleep," Dustin uttered. He lifted my legs to the couch, pushed my head to his thighs, and made sure it covered his opened jeans.

Panting from my hard work, I tried to regulate my breathing. I wasn't the best actor. When I tried for one of the main parts in school, I froze and ended up being a tree.

"Daddy?"

"Hey." Dustin cleared his throat since it sounded dry and like he'd done a marathon. "Hey, buddy. What are you doing up?"

"A dream. Has Miss Brooke gone?" I heard him approach closer.

"Shh, kiddo, she fell asleep."

Dear God, this was embarrassing. We'd nearly got caught. I felt like an asshole for starting this out in the damn living room and not somewhere private. But I honestly thought Benjie would have stayed asleep.

"Aww, she looks like Sleeping Beauty."

Dang it all, that was too sweet. But I was whorey Sleeping Beauty. Seriously, I had to be better than that and consider a child could wake up.

"That she does, buddy."

"Do you want to put her in my bed? I can sleep in with you. She must have been really tired."

"Like I thought you were, buddy."

"Yeah, until the dream woke me."

"How about you go get a glass of milk."

"I can pour it myself?" I could hear the shock and excitement in his voice.

"Go for it. Just be careful."

"Okay."

"Coast is clear," Dustin whispered.

Lifting my head, I went to sit, but Dustin picked that moment to do up his fly *with* my hair in it.

"My hair's stuck," I snapped low, panic closing around my chest. He tugged and pulled while I cringed.

"I can't get it out." Now he sounded panicked.

Even though fear gripped my gut, I couldn't stop the abrupt, slightly hysterical laugh, or the next words that flew out of my mouth, "That's what she said."

Dustin stilled and snorted.

A noise from the kitchen had me yanking my hair as the fear flew back inside me. "Just pull."

"Is this where I say, that's what he said?"

"Dustin," I whined. "Tug it out." I groaned when he snorted again.

"I don't want to hurt you."

"Dammit, Dustin, he'll come back in. Pull!"

Dustin yanked and my hair was free. There was a good chunk of my strands in the fly of his jeans, but he covered himself with his T-shirt. It was just in time for a little monster to come back into the living room.

"You're awake. Look, Miss Brooke, I poured my own glass." His little hand shook with how much milk was in the extra-large glass.

Clearing my throat, I felt my face heating when I gave Benjie two thumbs up. "Good job, little guy. But, ah, maybe only have a few sips."

"I will. Daddy said you fell asleep."

"I did. Must have been all that reading that made me tired." Standing, I stretched and rubbed at the back of my head. It was tender. "I better get going though."

"Why don't you stay the night? You can sleep in my bed and I'll go in with Daddy."

Why? Because I was still humiliated. We'd nearly been caught and it was my fault. I couldn't face Benjie in the morning, or Dustin.

"Um, thank you, but I really should get home."

"Why?"

"Because it'll be good to."

"Why?"

"Because, ah, I have to feed my kitten."

Shit, fuck, bastard. Why was that the only thing that popped into my head? I didn't have a kitten and I knew my screwup as soon as Benjie cried, "You have a kitten? I wanna see it. Please, please, please."

"Um, sure, one day soon, but it's a bit skittish with strangers." And now I was adding more lies to the first. I needed to get out of there before I said I had a damn farm or something.

"Benjie, take a few more sips of your drink and jump back into bed for me. I'm going to walk Brooke to the door. I just called a taxi."

Benjie sighed. "All right." He hugged half of me and quickly exited the room.

Silently, I grabbed my bag and walked to the front door. Opening it, I stepped out into the cool night air and shivered. My stomach tumbled in worry over what Dustin would think as he followed and shut the door behind him. On the stoop, we faced each other, and I swallowed thickly.

"I'm so sorry. I shouldn't have started that in the living room when Benjie could walk out and—" Dustin grabbed me before his lips slammed down on mine. His tongue invaded my mouth, but I was more than willing to play with his since it seemed he wasn't too upset about the scene.

He broke the kiss and said into my hair, "Never apologize for what you did. You'll learn we need to take every opportunity we can when kids are around. Hell, he could have easily walked into the bedroom. But we covered it well." He pulled back and winced, rubbing at the back of my head. "Sorry about your hair."

Smiling, since the worry had vanished, I shook my head. "It's fine."

He kissed my nose. "I didn't get to repay you. Promise, it'll be all about you next time."

Hugging him close, I kissed his neck. "I just wanted to give you something to remember while you're away."

"Darlin', I'll definitely remember that. Christ, I'm already looking forward to getting back." His arms tightened around my shoulders. "What are you doing tomorrow?"

"You have to pack and spend it with Benjie before you go. I'll be going out and buying a kitten."

Laughter roared out of him, until I covered his mouth and glanced to the door. Still chuckling, he asked, "Darlin', please don't tell me you're only buying a cat to please Benjie?"

"I lied, Dustin, and I hate that. I have to get a cat now so I'm not a liar. Besides, I can't exactly tell him it ran away or got hit by a car. Benjie would be devastated."

"He'll get over it."

Smacking Dustin's side, I shook my head. "I'm not doing that."

"You're serious? You'll go and buy a cat for my son?"

"Well, yes."

"Goddamn, Brooke, you're… amazing." He kissed my temple, my nose, cheek, and then my lips. "I better get back in there."

With another hug, I stepped back. "We'll talk soon."

He winked. "We will."

Dustin waited until I got into the taxi when it pulled up. Maybe a cat would be a good idea anyway because I was suddenly feeling lonely.

CHAPTER FIFTEEN

BROOKE

C an you tell me again why we're here?" Reagan asked, smirking as we entered the pet store.

Rolling my eyes, I poked her side. "I already told you."

"I know, but it's funny. You're really going to buy a kitten?"

"I am. Now help me pick one out. We'll need all the supplies as well." I headed for the area where they kept kittens. Opening the door, I walked in, and a gray and white cute little fluff ball raced up to me and pawed my shoes.

"Looks like you've been picked." Reagan smiled.

Grinning, I bent and picked the adorable monster up and it meowed at me. I clutched it gently to my chest and its tiny head rubbed against my chin. "I'm in love."

There were other kittens. Some playing, others trotted

over to check Reagan and me out, but I only had eyes for the one in my arms. The kitten started purring.

Yep, I was completely in love.

"Is it a boy or a girl?"

Glancing to Reagan, I laughed when I saw she had two kittens in her arms. "I don't know. But the question is, will I be the only one walking out of here with a kitten?"

Her face softened when she looked down at both. "I don't know." One lifted its paw and tapped her cheek. "Oh my God, I need to talk to Carter." She put them down and got out her phone while watching them stick close to her. "Carter, honey, how do you feel about kittens? ... Oh, you're a dog person?" She sounded gutted. "Where am I? Well, you see, when Brooke asked to have a coffee this morning, she actually took me to a pet shop because she promised Benjie he could see her new kitten when she didn't have one. ... Yes, I know, it made me laugh as well. ... Why did she do it? Because of a blow job."

"Ree!" I clipped.

Reagan cackled. "I'll tell you about it later. But I need you to know I've fallen in love. ... What? No, I wouldn't fall for another man. They're kittens. ... Yes, *they*, there's two who have claimed me. They want me to be their mommy, Carter. I can't walk away from them. If you say no, you'll have to come here and pry me away." Her eyes widened. "Wait, are you serious? ... Carter, are you sure? You know I was only joking when I said you'd have to pry me away? I don't mind if you say no." Tears filled her eyes. "God, I love you. You're the best in the whole world." She nodded, staring down at the two kittens who were still sticking close to her. "Okay, I'll see you soon. Think of some cute names. Bye, love you." When she hung up, she turned to me. "I'm getting kittens."

"I heard." I was more than happy with my monster who was now asleep in my arms. I doubted I could handle two of them.

The door behind us opened. "Hello, can I help you both today?" a woman in her late forties asked with a smile.

"Yes, please. I'd like to buy this little guy or girl, and Reagan would like those two."

"Wonderful. The one you're holding is a girl. The other two are a boy and a girl, but don't worry, all have already been fixed. How about you come out the front and we'll get the paperwork together? Then you can come collect them for their forever home."

"Sounds great. We'll also need to get some supplies," Reagan said.

"Perfect."

Not that I wanted to set my little girl down. I did, though, because the sooner I got the rest of the stuff out of the way, the quicker I could have her home.

The question was, what did I call her?

Fluffy wouldn't be enough.

Princess didn't seem right.

Maybe I had to wait until I saw her personality before I picked.

Hours later, I watched my kitten run across the floor after a ball, knock into a plant, then bounce off it before she hit her head into the couch.

No one told me they were full of energy.

No one told me how much you feared they got hurt or

stood on or could slip out the front or back door while you weren't watching. I'd thought I'd lost her when I went outside to the clothesline. My neighbors probably thought I was a crazy lady calling "Pussy," all over the place. In the end, I found her curled up under my curtain in the front living room window, sound asleep.

My heart was still racing.

Bending, I picked her up and checked her head. "You're such a hooligan. How were you so sweet at the store and here you're ready to tear into everything?" Bringing her to my chest, I glanced around at the mess. Toys littered the floor, as well as the mess from the trash can, which she got into when I didn't have the lid on properly.

She started purring in my arms, and once again, I was back in love and saying, "Who cares about the mess." Kissing the top of her head, I wondered aloud, "What will I call you? It'll need to be something Benjie and Dustin like." She rubbed into me again and then attacked my hand when I went to pet her. Smiling, I played with her while I thought some more about it. "What about Wiggles?" I mused, since her butt kept wiggling in the air. But she didn't look up at that. "Smooches? Nope. Izzy? No again. Valkyrie?" She stopped attacking me for a moment and looked up. "You like that one? We can use Val for short, but you'll be known as Valkyrie."

It was perfect since she seemed like a little warrior.

Later, when I was sitting on the couch and trying to tell Val off for attacking my sock-covered toes, my phone rang.

Picking it up, I saw Dustin's name and smiled. "Hi. What are you doing up so late?"

"Just got into the hotel, darlin'. Sorry I couldn't text earlier. Your kitty is cute."

I smiled. "Thank you. Her name is Valkyrie. But Val for short. She's a little shit, but worth it because she has her cute moments."

"Have I said you're amazing?"

"You have. But seriously, I should have had a pet a long time ago. She's good company when she's not up to mischief."

"Can't wait to actually meet her. Did you organize a day with Benjie?"

"I spoke to Emily just before and I'll pick Benjie up the day after tomorrow. I'm looking forward to them meeting."

"He'll love her."

"I figured as much. She's impossible not to love. How have you been though? Didn't you have a photo shoot today?"

"Yeah, just like any other time."

"Has North reached out?"

"No, darlin', and I'm not pushing."

"That's probably wise. What's your plan for tomorrow?"

"Some interviews. Boring shit that comes with playing football. Seems like I haven't seen you in ages, darlin'. Already missing you."

My body warmed, and my mind went to Dustin's gorgeous cock in my mouth.

"Same."

"Looking forward to returning the favor, darlin'. It's been on my mind every second of the day. Can't wait to get a taste of you, sweetheart." He hummed under his breath, and my nipples perked up while my belly fluttered to life with a thousand butterflies.

It was suddenly hard to catch a breath because that image was stuck in my brain.

I could hear the humor in his voice when he said, "You still there, darlin'?"

"Yes," I squeaked and immediately cringed. Clearing my throat as he chuckled low through the phone, which didn't help because his voice was like a wet dream, I went on to say, "I'm, ah, here."

"Are you thinking about it, darlin'?"

Rubbing my thighs together, I realized he needed to stop talking or I was going to stick my hand down my pants.

"Dustin, you need to stop talking."

Another low chuckle sounded, and I bit my bottom lip while Dustin tsked. "Brooke, am I getting to you, darlin'?"

"Yes. Now quit it."

"Or I could help relieve some tension."

My throat felt thick as I swallowed. "Sorry?" I breathed.

"Put your kitty to bed, babe, and call me back. I'll be on my bed waiting for you. Hell, I'll even send you a photo."

"A-Are we really doing this?"

"Yeah, darlin'. Need to hear you come when we talk."

"Dustin," I whispered. Was it too soon? Heck, I hadn't thought so when I had his dick in my mouth. But this seemed more intimate. *And what, a dick in your mouth isn't?*

"I need this, darlin'. I wanna feel close to you when I can't reach you. Let me give this to you, baby."

Biting my bottom lip, I nodded. "Okay."

"Call me back as soon as you're in bed."

"I will."

"Good."

When the call ended, I gnawed on my bottom lip some more and watched as Val started to curl up for a sleep. At least she was ready for bed and wouldn't interrupt what Dustin had planned. An excited thrill swept over me despite my nerves. Standing, I pocketed my phone and picked Val up. I'd bought a playpen with a roof for her to sleep in because at the shop I'd been worried she'd end up hurting herself through the night when I wouldn't be watching her.

In my room, I placed her in her bed and double-checked she had water, toys, and the extra container of kitty litter.

Kissing the top of her head, I told her, "Be a good girl while Mommy gets off with her boyfriend." I groaned because that just sounded so wrong.

After Val was situated, I went into the bathroom and got ready for bed. My heart wouldn't quit racing, and even my hands shook a little from the nervous energy flowing through me. I'd never had phone sex and wasn't sure I'd be any good at it.

Sighing, I braced my hands on the bathroom basin and stared at myself in the mirror.

Did I need to put on more makeup? What was I supposed to wear? Something sexy or just go for naked?

Not knowing sent my stomach into a spiral. I felt like throwing up.

Right. I could do this.

Straightening, I stalked back into the bedroom to place my phone on the bed and undressed before I pulled open a drawer to my bedside table. Red always looked nice on me. I took out my favorite piece of lingerie that popped the girls up nicely and hugged my waist. I slipped into the matching panties and climbed into bed. I pulled the blankets up to my waist and grabbed my phone.

My breath shuddered out of me as I stared at the blank screen.

I could do this.

I could. For Dustin... and for me.

Blowing out a breath, I unlocked the screen and went to Dustin's name in the call log. Before I chickened out, I pressed and waited.

It rang once. "Darlin', I was just about to send you a photo."

"Photos aren't safe, honey. We could do a video call. That's if you want to. We don't—" The option to switch to a video chat rang and I pressed the button.

On the screen I saw Dustin's smirking face before it died and he choked out, "What are you wearing?"

"Something." I smiled. Seeing his reaction helped my nerves settle a little in my stomach. I didn't feel as cold once his eyes ran over every inch of the top half of me.

"You look gorgeous, darlin'."

"Thank you," I whispered, shyness coming over me, but I wasn't going to let that stop this from happening. "Show me you."

He chuckled. "Do I get a reward if I do?"

Winking, I dipped the phone down a little before I pulled it back up to my face. "You might."

"Jesus. I'm not sure this'll be good for my heart."

Laughing, I shook my head. "Says the man who works out twice a day and plays football. I think you'll be fine."

"True, and I do want to see more." He grinned and then

slowly his phone moved from just his face down to his neck. Then his chest and shoulders came into view and finally his abs. I knew he was fit. But I didn't know he was *F I T* fit. I gulped and felt like I had to push my eyes back in my head.

Dustin was made of perfection. His skin was smooth, and I wanted to run my tongue and teeth over every inch, to mark him in ways only I could.

"Even your nipples are perfect."

His body moved with his laughter, and I enjoyed watching the movement.

Veins popped in his arms, and I wished I was there to nibble on them. I wanted to kiss him all over.

His face was in view once more. I pouted. "No fair. That wasn't long enough."

He snorted. "It was when I haven't seen all of you yet. Give me the goods, sweetheart."

I bit my bottom lip, a flash of worry sweeping through me over the thought of what I would do if Dustin didn't like all of me? I wasn't slim. I had a belly that jiggled.

"Whatever you're thinking, stop. I don't like the look in your eyes, darlin'. You have nothing to worry about. I know I'm going to love everything I see. Hell, I'm already hard from everything I've seen so far. Please don't question my attraction to you."

"Okay," I uttered. Flicking the blanket off me, I slowly ran the phone down over my body. I heard his sharp intake of breath, his moan, and when he clipped, "Fuck me," he groaned. "Shit, Brooke. I'm not going to last."

My eyes rounded. "Wait, you're already touching yourself?" I pulled the phone up to my face and slipped a hand into my panties.

"I am. You can't expect me not to when I saw what I wanted in front of me. Christ, darlin', I can't wait to touch you. To taste every inch. To kiss, bite, and run my hands over your sexy-as-fuck body."

"Dustin," I breathed. How could I already be close? It was his voice. His damn rough and hot voice.

"Are you touching yourself, darlin'?"

"Yes." I nodded, biting my bottom lip.

"Show me your hand in there, Brooke. Need to see it."

Lowering the phone, I hoped I had the camera in the right spot, and from the groan Dustin let out, I did, but I was too busy closing my eyes and getting off on the sounds Dustin made—on his voice, his words. "Hell, darlin', I bet you're wet. So wet. Goddamn, I want to taste you. I'd lick your pussy all over but pay special attention to your clit while I slowly glided a finger inside of you."

"God, Dustin."

"Yeah, sweetheart, that's exactly what you'd say with me between your legs."

Legs that shook a little from the pleasure running through me.

"That's it, darlin', go faster. Imagine me between your thighs. You wouldn't be able to move your hips like that, baby. Not when I was there holding onto them while my tongue tasted you."

"I-I'm close."

"So am I, darlin'. I'm so fucking hard from looking at you pleasuring yourself. It's an amazing sight."

"I wanna see you come."

"After you're done, baby. I already know I'm going to come long and hard from watching you. I wish those were my fingers in your panties. I wish I was lying next to you so I could be the one feeling your tight, wet pussy. I want—"

"Dustin," I cried, shattering around my fingers while I rubbed the heel of my palm onto my clit.

"Yes, darlin'. Keep coming for me." He groaned long and loud.

And I was.

My legs shook, my body ignited all over.

The phone dropped. I quickly picked it up and brought it up to my face, which I knew was turning red. "Your turn."

"Too late, darlin'." He smirked. "I couldn't stop coming when you did." The view on his phone dipped to his stomach and chest, where I saw his cum pooling over it.

"Not fair."

He chuckled, bringing the screen back up to his face. "There'll be plenty more times to see it. In person too."

"I can't wait, honey."

His gaze warmed. "Love hearing that from you, darlin'. Now, you ready to sleep?"

"Oh yeah. You've exhausted me."

He grinned and it looked a little cocky. "Same, darlin'. I'll talk to you soon. Have sweet dreams of me."

Saluting him, I winked. "I'll try."

Okay, for my first time at phone sex, I was sure things went really well, but still I couldn't wait until Dustin was right there beside me.

CHAPTER SIXTEEN

DUSTIN

*O*rth didn't room with me like usual. I didn't know whose room he'd been in either. He seemed to be quick at disappearing, like he was Superman or something. It wasn't until the fourth night he headed my way. "Yo, room with me?"

I glanced all around me to see if he was talking to me or someone else. Then, just to be a smartass, I pointed at my chest. "Are you talking to me?" I clasped my hands in front of me and jumped up and down a little. "OMG, is North Harrison talking to little old me?"

He glared, but his lips twitched. "Don't be a dick. Can you or not?"

"Sure. I've been taking a single room, but I'm willing to share a double room with you since you asked me so nicely."

He nodded and hooked his bag over his shoulder before he followed me into the hotel. Coach was there handing out keys, and I stopped in front of him just as Jennings did.

Shit.

"Single or double? I have one of each left."

"I'll take a double," Jennings said.

Oh fuck.

"I'm roomin' with Grant," North supplied.

Jennings's jaw clenched. He handed the key over to me with a glare that threatened to set me on fire before taking the other key from Coach and stalking toward the elevators.

As North and I followed slowly behind, I prayed the doors would open before we got there to take Jennings up to whatever floor. If not, I was afraid for my life.

Leaning toward North, I asked, "How many ways will he be thinking of killing me?"

North snorted. "Won't be you. It'll be me, and about fifty."

Of course, my luck was out the window, because by the time we reached the elevator, the doors hadn't opened so we stood there awkwardly together. I rocked back and forth on my feet and adjusted my bag over my shoulder.

Was it suddenly hot?

Sweat formed on my neck and hands. Especially when I caught Jennings eyeing me like he wanted to choke me.

"Ah, good weather we're having." The lame words left my mouth.

Jennings just stared his hatred my way, while North snorted.

"Say, uh, North, you remember my girlfriend, Brooke?"

North grunted. I took it as a yes.

"Yeah, well, she just picked up a kitten the other day."

Thank fuck the doors opened. I nearly fell on my face with how quickly I moved in. My luck was still in the gutter when I noted we were on the same floor, and it was on the twentieth level. Just a nice little ride with a murderous man and one who was now answering in snorts and grunts.

Fun times.

Tugging at the collar of my tee, I cleared my suddenly dry throat.

Both of them looked at me, and I instantly regretted gaining their attention.

"Do we need to hug something out?"

"What the fuck?" Jennings snarled.

Taking a step back, I shrugged. "You know the saying if two people are upset about something it's best to hug it out?" I glanced to North and found him staring at me like I'd grown another head. "Never heard it?"

North turned to Jennings. "You don't need to talk to him like that."

Jennings straightened and stepped into North's space. I wanted to vanish into the floor.

"Are you telling me what to do?"

"Maybe if I did, you'd get that stick outta your ass."

I coughed, since my perverted mind went to North being up Jennings's ass. It was lucky I didn't say anything.

Jennings's jaw clenched. "Stop trying to save me."

"Fine," North drew out.

Where was some popcorn when I needed it?

Praise Jesus, the doors dinged open, and I fled into the hallway. I'd let them sort it out. No way was I getting in the middle of that. It also seemed North could handle Jennings's asshole attitude. Once at the room, I swiped the key in the lock and pushed it open. I didn't step through though.

"North," I heard and glanced down over to see North was getting close to our room. Jennings had stopped at a room down the hall. "North." Jennings scowled when North ignored him and nodded at me to get in the room.

I did.

It didn't surprise me when North dumped his bag in there and grabbed the room key from my hand before he shut the door again with him on the outside.

"Holy fucking shit." That was intense. Dropping my bag on the bed away from the door, I pulled out my phone and hit Brooke's number.

"Hello?"

"I nearly died tonight."

"What? Are you okay? Oh God, I'll get on a plane right now. Where are you? Are you in the hospital? Dustin? Are you okay?"

Maybe it would have been better if I led with something else.

"Darlin', sorry to have scared you. I'm okay. I didn't nearly die."

Silence, then I heard a door slam and winced. Had she been literally walking out the door to come to me?

"Brooke? Sweetheart?"

"I'm going to kill you myself." She took a loud breath. "What the fuck were you thinking saying that? I walked out of my house in panties, Dustin. Panties."

Now there was a pleasant image. Until I thought of another prick seeing her.

"Please tell me no one saw you and you're back inside."

"I don't know, and I am. But seriously, Dustin, I'm going to kick your ass when you get home."

"I'll even let you, darlin'. I wasn't thinking, but my death could have been close."

"How?" she demanded. "And it better be good."

Wincing, I scrubbed a hand over my face and sat on the end of the bed. "North hasn't really approached or talked to me. Until tonight. He asked to share a room, but I'm pretty sure Jennings wanted to share with him. Darlin', I'd be dead if Jennings had anything to do with it. Do you know how fucking awkward the elevator ride up was? I asked them if they needed to hug it out because the tension in there was damn thick. I'll have to sleep with one eye open in case Jennings sneaks into the room and decides to kill me in my sleep."

Brooke snorted. "You're exaggerating."

"I'm not. Seriously, I'm still sweating from the situation. If I don't speak to you tomorrow, just know I've loved our time together and give Benjie lots of hugs."

Her laughter rang through the phone. "I really should stay mad at you, but I can't seem to and it's not fair."

"I'm just too cute."

"You're definitely something."

"Can we get back to the fact you were only in panties to begin with? Why?"

"Nothing exciting, if that's where your mind was going, and knowing you, it probably was. Val decided to throw up on me and the bed. I had just got out of my pajamas when you called and scared the hell out of me."

Wincing, I rubbed at the back of my neck. "Sorry again about that."

The door to the room opened, and North, with a sour look on his face, entered. He threw the key card down on the table and flopped onto the bed.

"North?" I called.

He grunted.

"Can you tell Brooke how close I was to death? I may have scared her a little."

He groaned and rolled over to sit up. "You told your woman you were close to death because of Jennings?"

I nodded.

North sighed. "Brooke," he said louder. I put it on speaker. "Grant was being a big baby and can't handle a little intimidation."

"I was not," I yelled. "He's lying, darlin'. I really won't get a lick of sleep tonight thinking Jennings will break in here and murder me."

North rolled his eyes and lay back down.

Brooke, laughing once again, said, "I better let you go do some bonding with your friend. Sleep well, sunshine. I'm sure you won't wake to find Jennings standing over you."

North chuckled.

"That's cruel, woman."

"Thank you. Goodnight."

"Night, darlin'. Good luck with your pussy."

"Dustin!"

"Jesus," North grumbled.

"It's a kitten, North. There is nothing sexual in that statement."

"This is Grant we're talkin' about. You'll learn his mind's always in the gutter."

Brooke huffed. "I already figured it out. Bye."

"Bye," we both said before I hung up.

North sat back up and rubbed a hand over his face. "She's good for you."

I smiled. "Yeah, she is. Benjie adores her also."

"Good to see you happy, man."

Thinning my lips, I wondered if now would be a good time to have a chat.

When I opened my mouth, North's hand rose. "Nope. Don't go there."

Sighing, I kicked off my shoes and slid onto the bed more. "I thought we were friends. It's been you, me, and Carter for a long time, North. Why can't I question my friend about things in his life? I could help, you know."

His brow rose.

"I could." I waited, but he said no more and instead removed his shoes and got up from the bed to grab his bag.

"Do you know you're calling me Grant instead of Dustin? I know someone else who does that."

"*Dustin.* Don't."

"Fine. I'm going to call room service. Do you want anything?"

"Yeah. Whatever you grab, I'll have." He dumped his bag on the bed and unzipped it, taking some clothes out. He paused, staring down at the bed. "I don't know what's goin' on with Jennings and me."

"It's okay not to know. As long as he's treating you right."

He made a noise in the back of his throat. "He does. But… it's hard because he's so closed off. Shit, I didn't know I was into guys until him, but he's further in the closet than I am, and he's always known he was gay."

"You don't want to hide, but he does?" I guessed.

"Yeah, somethin' like that. He's got a shit father who's against it." He turned and eyed me. "Are you cool with this shit?"

"What? With you being into guys?"

"Yeah."

"North, my heart breaks a little you'd question me like that. I love you like a brother from another mother no matter who you do."

He snorted, then chuckled. "You're a dickhead." He made his way to the bathroom.

"A dickhead who loooooves you."

He shot me the middle finger over his shoulder. But at the door to the bathroom, he turned. "Jennings won't say or do shit to you. He's just scared you'll say somethin' to the team or management. I've told him you wouldn't do that. You or Carter."

"Damn right we won't."

He nodded. "I know."

"What's up with the space though? Not that I don't love having you around. But did you two get into a fight last night?"

"I wasn't in his room since we've been away. I wasn't ready to talk to you, sorry. So, I got a single room on my own to think. We fought the night you guys rocked up and haven't really talked since, or until before, but even then he was just saying shit about you and Carter spreading rumors. When he's an idiot like that, not trusting me in knowing you guys, I don't want anythin' to do with him."

"You like him. Like *really* like him?"

North's brows drew together as he shook his head. "You sound like a thirteen-year-old."

"So? Just answer the question. Does he make you happy? Do you get butterflies over the guy? Can you see a future with him?"

He groaned and glared at me. "Do you feel all those things with Brooke?"

"Yes. Do you with Jennings?"

His tone was soft. "Yeah." He shook his head again. "But enough of this shit. I'm goin' for a shower."

Saluting him, I grabbed the room's phone. "I'll get the food ready, and we can watch some emotional movie and eat while we cry."

"Fucking dick," he muttered, but I caught his smile before he closed the door.

I quickly placed an order and then sat back, contemplating whether it was best I stayed out of North's business or not.

More importantly, did I risk my life by going to talk to Jennings?

I had Brooke and Benjie to think about.

Christ, I was being a pussy.

When I heard the shower switch on, I climbed off the bed and grabbed the room key. Quietly, I got out the door and moved down the few doors to Jennings's room. I didn't know if it was hunger pains in my gut or if I was about to shit myself from nerves.

Man the fuck up, I told myself before I reached out and knocked on the door.

It took a couple of beats, just enough time for sweat to pool at the base of my neck, before the door swung open aggressively and Jennings stood in it, glowering.

"Is that expression the only one you have?" When Jennings stepped forward, I shot my hand up in front of me. "Shit, I didn't mean it. Don't kill me. North will cry."

His brow rose. "North is right. You're like a little yippy puppy."

"He said that about me? Aw, that's kind of cute."

"And annoying."

Shrugging, I threw out a hand. "I don't see it that way. Anyway, I only have a few moments before North gets out of the shower. I want you to know that Carter and I would never say anything about what we saw because North is our friend. We respect his privacy—"

"Except when barging into his house."

"That was different. He'd been ignoring us so we're going to worry about him. Now we know he was busy with you, it explains things." I glanced down the hall and back again. "Look, I promise nothing will come from Carter and me or our women. But I need you to understand that if you hurt North, we *will* fuck you up, even though you scare the shit out of us. He's never liked someone like he has you. Shit, you give him all those gooey feelings, but right now you're fucking up. Don't let outside crap come between you and him if he's important to you. If he's not important, then let him know so he can move on."

His jaw clenched and he fisted his hands at his sides. He didn't like the idea of North moving on. Good.

"All right, I'm out. Later."

Starting to walk off, I stopped when I heard, "Grant." Glancing over my shoulder, I tipped my chin up to him to keep going. He sighed. "Thanks for coming to talk to me."

Spinning, I clasped my hands in front of me. "Does this mean we can be friends?"

His look of horror amused me too much. If he stuck around, it'd be fun giving this guy shit.

"I... don't know what to fucking say." He shook his head, stepped back into his room, and shut the door.

"It's okay," I called. "We'll work on it, bestie." My work here was done. Now he'd better get his head out of his ass and make my friend as happy as I was.

CHAPTER SEVENTEEN

BROOKE

*D*ustin was on his way to my house. There was no
way I could contain the fluttering in my stomach
or chest.

I was going to get me some, and I couldn't wait.

Walking through the house, I made sure things were tidy
before I slipped into my bedroom and stood in my walk-in
closet, staring at my clothes. I'd already changed into jeans
and a dark blue shirt, but I wasn't happy with my choice, yet I
didn't see anything else I wanted to wear.

What would Dustin do if I opened the door naked?

Did I dare?

Cackling to myself, I shook the idea out of my head just in
case it didn't end up being Dustin knocking on my door.

What about lingerie with a robe over it?

Nope, I didn't want to jump right into sexy time. Dustin could be exhausted from traveling or hungry. Heck, there was a chance he might not want to do anything in the first place. I hoped not, but I wouldn't jump his bones if he wasn't ready for it.

Well, I'd try not to. But having phone sex a couple more nights had really amped up my drive for the man. He'd even kept me on a video chat while he'd showered, and that image played on repeat in my mind a lot.

It wasn't something I could think of now though. I had to make sure everything was ready, which meant me also. Since no other clothes were jumping out at me, I went back out into the living room to find Val chasing after a ball.

In the kitchen, I checked the risotto and turned down the heat a little. All right, I didn't make the risotto since I was useless in the kitchen. Regan had come over earlier to prepare it, and all I had to do was cook it. Something I could manage. I hoped. A timer went off, which told me the cookies were ready. I reset it for the risotto. The cookies were at least something I could handle. I took them out of the oven and slid them onto the cooling rack before dropping the sheet in the sink. Glancing around, I realized I looked like a domesticated housewife, waiting for her husband to return home.

Smiling, my body warmed at the idea. I wasn't thinking of marriage or anything to tie Dustin down. We were only starting out, but I could still enjoy the idea of being his housewife.

A knock on the door pumped my blood through my veins quicker, and my fluttering shot up to a storm as I made my way to the front door.

Val had disappeared somewhere because she didn't like when people knocked on the door; it scared the crap out of her. Thankfully, not literally.

There wasn't a chance I could wipe the crazy excited smile off my face. My breath whooshed out of me when I opened the door and saw Dustin standing there with a bag slung over his shoulder.

He was here.

Right here in front of me, and he looked godly in his suit.

"Wait, a suit?"

"Came from an interview, darlin'." He stepped in, dropped his bag, and wound his arms around my waist. "Come here." I managed to push the door closed before I wrapped my arms around his neck and got to my tippy-toes as our lips crashed together.

Dustin ran his hands down to my ass and gripped, but they didn't stay there. He smoothed them back up to cup my breasts as our kiss of teasing, demanding, and tasting went on and on.

A timer rang through the house. Dustin broke the kiss with a groan. "Are you trying to cook? Do we need the fire station on hold?"

Smacking his arm, I glared. "I wish Nana never said anything to you."

He tugged me close and kissed my temple. "But teasing you is so much fun."

"Then I should have answered the door naked to tease you."

His groan sounded painful. He thrust his erection into my

hip. "It wouldn't have been safe for you. I would have mauled you on the front stoop."

"Yes, but that's where the teasing part comes in. I wouldn't have let you."

He brushed a couple of fingers down the side of my face. "Then you would have seen my first tantrum."

Laughing, I shook my head and hugged him close. "It's good to have you here instead of on the phone."

"I agree, darlin'." He kissed my shoulder. "Now, can dinner hold because I'm a guy who likes dessert first?"

Lifting my gaze, I knew it would hold desire. "What's for dessert? The cookies I made or—"

"You," he growled out before picking me up into his arms, his hands on my ass. His bulge rubbed in the right spot when he started down the hallway.

"Shit, wait. I need to turn off dinner." He let me go and I bolted for the kitchen. "You get naked and ready for me, please."

His chuckle hit me before I made it into the kitchen and turned off the pot, moving it aside. I hoped it didn't get ruined, since Reagan had worked hard on the meal for us. Though, if it was, I'd be okay with that.

Racing back down the hall, I found Dustin— "You're not naked." Instead, he stood beside the bed with Val in his arms, petting her.

He grinned. "She's adorable."

Softening, because who wouldn't when their man held a kitten gently to him, I smiled. "She is. I told you how much Benjie loved her, so don't be surprised if he begs for one. He already has with Emily."

"I guess he'll have to come around more often." He winked. "At least it'll be an excuse to see you."

"I'm all for that plan."

"Good. Is that her bed?" He nodded to the playpen.

"It is."

After he had her situated, he slipped by me with a kiss on my neck. "I'm just going to wash my hands."

An excited, yet nervous, yip noise escaped me. He must have taken it as a yes because he kept going with a chuckle. As soon as he stepped into the bathroom, I quickly removed my shirt, then undid my jeans and shoved them down my legs, stepping out of them. It left me in my bra and panties. I hoped it wasn't too forward, but he did say he wanted dessert first.

What did I do now though?

Did I pose? I tried a few and it made me look like a douche. Moving to the bed, I sat on the edge, but I looked down and saw those few extra rolls. I scrunched my gut lower to pop a few more out and then laughed to myself.

Yeah, that was appealing.

Groaning, I went to stand, until I heard, "Do not move."

Slowly, I lifted my gaze to Dustin's heated one, as he leaned against the doorframe. My eyes flashed wide. "How long have you been standing there?"

His lips twitched. "One of my favorite poses was with your hand on the bed and ass in the air." My face burned. He stalked toward me and removed his tee. "However, I do like this one."

Drawing my brows down in confusion, I glanced down to myself. All I was doing was sitting on the bed. How could he like this one?

Dustin suddenly stopped in front of me, dropped to his knees, and gripped my thighs before he spread my legs. My heart jumped into my throat as tiny Tinkerbells flew around inside my stomach. My nipples wouldn't be outdone though. They hardened, and my pussy clenched.

Dustin slid a hand up my thigh, drawing a shudder from me. I bit my bottom lip and watched him draw closer, until he brushed two fingers up and down the crotch of my panties.

My skin broke out in goose bumps, and I rocked forward a little. His smirk was sexy. "Yeah, I definitely like this." His fingers pressed in more as he rubbed them up and down. A whimper escaped me. "I've been thinking about you nonstop while away. You've got me addicted, Brooke Baker."

"So have you," I breathed, resting my hands on the bed behind me while he kept up his seductive massage.

"Lift your hips, darlin'. I've got to have a taste."

"Are you sure—"

"Shut it and lift." His hands went to my panties at my hips, and when I lifted, he dragged them down over my ass and legs. I'd closed my legs when he dropped my panties to the floor, but Dustin's hands were back on my knees and spreading them apart with a slightly annoyed lift to his brow when I tried to keep them closed.

When he had them open, he dove in before I could do anything, and on the first lick from bottom to top, I gripped the blankets and arched up into his mouth. "Dustin," I whispered.

"Fuck, darlin'." It was all he said before it felt like he locked his mouth onto my pussy and licked, sucked, nipped, and teased in all the right places. I'd had men and women pleasure me this way before, but none of them had driven me wild where I couldn't catch a breath like Dustin was.

"D-Dustin." I dropped back on the bedding, closing my eyes, and let the pleasure fill my entire body. When he inserted a finger and curled it up inside me while he tongued and sucked on my clit, I lost it. Crying his name, my pussy clamped down on his finger that still moved, and he drew out a strong orgasm from me.

Breathing heavily, I blinked up at the ceiling as my soul joined back within my body. Dustin pressed a kiss to my mound as he withdrew his finger, causing me to shudder. His hands massaged my thighs as I slowly sat up. The cocky smile on his face had my face heating.

"Yeah, yeah, you're all-powerful and mighty." I waved a hand around.

Dustin chuckled. "Make sure to remember it, darlin'."

"I might, but only in the bedroom." My gaze ran down his exquisite body. His jeans seemed tighter in the crotch area. "Let me help you remove those pesky pants."

He cocked a brow. "You're still able to function after my powerful and mighty work? I must be losing my powers."

Snorting, I shook my head and smiled. "My legs might take some time to work, but my hands are good." Dustin stood between my legs. Reaching out, I undid the button, then the zipper, and hooked my thumbs in the side of his jeans as I dragged them down. His cock sprang free and bobbed in front of me. I hadn't even gotten his jeans all the way down before I dipped forward and sucked him into my mouth while I grabbed his ass cheeks and tugged him closer.

"Jesus, fuck," he clipped. He threaded his fingers into my

hair, and with the other hand, he used his thumb to trace around my lips that glided up and down his hard cock.

Dark eyes peered down at me before he moved his gaze to his thumb, which he pushed into my mouth as he drew his dick all the way out. His jaw clenched and he let out a string of curses when I kept sucking and flicking my tongue around his thumb.

"Stand up, darlin'."

My legs were a little shaky when I stood. I ran my hands up and over all of Dustin's muscles, amazed at how hard and beautiful they were.

Dustin dipped to gently rub his nose against mine before he captured my lips in a mind-spinning kiss. When he pulled back and said, "No condom?" my pussy clenched.

I nodded, pressing my lips to his chest. "No condom."

"Fuck, this might not last then."

Laughing lightly, I lifted my gaze to his. "Don't worry, you're still almighty to me."

His grin was big, but it dropped away when he ordered, "Turn around. Knees on the edge of the bed and show me that ass."

My belly fluttered along with my heart. Dustin's hands ran over my body as I turned slowly and got my knees to the bed.

Dustin sucked in a sharp breath while he ran both hands over the globes of my cheeks, then up and down my back and hips.

"Goddamn, darlin', you're gorgeous." A finger slid inside me, and I gasped. "This is all mine."

I hummed.

"No, sweetheart, tell me it's mine." He withdrew his finger

and pushed back in. I whimpered and dropped to my elbows on the bed.

Glancing over my shoulder, I told him, "Yours, all yours."

"Damn right." He slapped a hand down on my ass. I cried out and pushed back on his finger and hand.

"Dustin, please."

"You want my cock?"

"Yes!"

"How much do you want it?" His tone was rough, hard, and I liked it a lot. Even when he wasn't giving me what I wanted and kept teasing.

"Dustin," I snapped.

Finally, he removed the finger, and the tip of his warm dick pressed against my entrance.

"How much, Brooke?" He didn't push in. Instead, he just kept it there, and when I tried to move back onto it, he gripped my hips and held me in place.

Letting out a frustrated breath, I peered over my shoulder and glared. Only he was busy watching his hands and between his legs. Sweat coated his brow, so I knew he was having a hard time holding back.

"Dustin, I want your cock more than anything right now."

He smiled and caught my gaze. "That'a girl." His thrust had me dropping my forehead to my arms and moaning as he filled me completely.

"All right?"

"Oh yeah," I answered.

"Fuck, so perfect for me." He rested over me, his hands gliding up to cup my breasts. "Christ, darlin'. You're amazing."

"Then fuck me, honey."

He groaned into my shoulder and rolled my breasts around in his hands. "I will. Just give me a second. You're damn tight, sweetheart. I don't want it to end just yet."

A giggle escaped me, but when he pulled out and thrust back in, the laughter faded, and my vision wavered. He kissed my shoulder again before he stood behind me and pressed his hands to my hips, gripping.

"Ready, darlin'?"

"Yes." I moaned as Dustin pulled out and pushed in. Getting to my hands, I rocked back harder on his thrusts. Sounds I'd never made before left me.

"Brooke, baby, you feel fucking amazing. Christ, I-I can't slow down, darlin'."

"N-Next time," I reassured him, right before his hips slapped into my ass. His dick pistoned in and out of me, and I panted out my moans as my lower belly tingled. "Dustin, God, yes."

His heat hit my back, but he kept filling me in and out even as he kissed my shoulder and neck. "So good. Close."

Knowing it was driving him crazy like it was me and having the feel of him bare inside threw me over the edge. He groaned low and long as my pussy tightened around him, and I whimpered out his name.

"Darlin', yes, fuck yes." A grunted groan dropped from his mouth on my shoulder. He stilled for a second before his thrusts grew wild, and I felt him swell before his hot seed filled me. He slowed, lifting off me, but he didn't stop running his hand over me while he was still planted inside me.

"I'll never get enough of touching you."

Licking my suddenly dry lips, I glanced over. "I'll never get enough of you fucking me."

He groaned, jaw clenched. "Need a minute to go again, darlin'."

"So... you're not almighty?"

A cry escaped me when he slapped a hand to my ass, then rubbed the spot. "I still am." He pulled out and shifted back a little. I went to move to go clean up, but his hands on my back and hip stilled me. Then two of his fingers filled me.

I moaned. "Dustin."

"Like seeing my cum in you, darlin'. Like it very much."

Dear God, I'd lied. He was almighty because that line had me tingling all over.

Wetness coated my thigh as he played with his cum in my pussy. His teeth nipped at my ass cheek before he kissed there.

"Can't wait to see it again and again and again." He slipped his fingers free and helped me stand before him. I ran my hands over his chest, but my eyes widened when he cupped my pussy with a hand. "But for now, I'm going to clean you up a little but not all the way because while we have dinner, I want to know a part of me is still inside you. All right?"

Nodding, I leaned into him and kissed his chest as desire hit me right in the belly and my body shivered. "Okay," I whispered.

It was easy to say Dustin and I were definitely made for each other in the bedroom. At least I wouldn't have to break up with him... though, even if he hadn't been godly, there was a chance I would have kept him around. He'd kinda grown on me, like a lot. My heart seemed to beat in a different way whenever I thought about him or when he was near.

CHAPTER EIGHTEEN

DUSTIN

*B*rooke was asleep in my bed, and I couldn't stop staring at her like a creep. We'd been sneaking around for a couple of months, and I was tired of hiding it from Benjie, especially as it meant Brooke had to leave each night—or sneak away first thing in the morning—when my son was home.

It was time to tell him.

Our relationship was strong, and I couldn't imagine my life without Brooke in it.

I wanted to wake up every morning like—

Oh fuck, it was morning and Benjie was here. Brooke was going to freak the hell out her alarm hadn't gone off.

Yet, I couldn't find the will to care too much. I mean, it

wasn't the best way for Benjie to find out about me and Brooke, but it needed to happen.

Tucking her hair behind her ear, I chuckled when she swatted my hand away and groaned sleepily. "No, you had me twice, and I love your cock, but I need sleep."

"I noticed your love for my cock, but I need you—"

Her hand covered my mouth, even while she kept her eyes closed. "Your cock isn't the only thing I love."

My heart shimmied inside my chest. I took her wrist, kissed her palm, but pulled her hand away. "What are you saying, darlin'?"

She peeked out as a blush spread across her cheeks. "I *might* love you too."

A smile formed on my lips. "Might?"

"Okay, I *could* love you too if you let me sleep."

I growled in the back of my throat and rolled into her so she had to fall from her side to her back. "Could? Say it, darlin'. Let me hear it."

She grinned up at me and cupped my cheeks. "I do love you, Dustin Grant."

There went my heart again, dancing for her. Only my gut tangoed along with it. Leaning down, I kissed her nose. "I love you too, Brooke Baker."

Her eyes flared a little. "You do?"

"I do. Which is why we need to tell Benjie about this."

Her arms wrapped around my neck, and she pulled me down for a hot and heavy kiss. One that distracted me and had me grinding my hard dick into her hip.

The kiss trailed off into small pecks before I moved my lips down to her neck and sucked. A shuddered breath left her as she ran her hands up and down my back. I loved that even out of bed, Brooke was a touchy person. She sought me out with her hands or mouth all the time. It was good, as I was an affectionate person as well.

But then she stilled under me.

"Dustin?"

"Hmm?" I kissed the mark on her neck.

"Is it morning?"

"Yeah, I tried telling you— Ooof." Brooke shoved me hard off her and I caught an elbow to the gut.

She quickly climbed out of bed, while I lay on my side and watched her, palming my aching dick. She stopped moving to watch me, then shot me a glare. "Don't distract me. I can't believe I didn't wake up. Did I set my alarm? I would have. You didn't turn it off, did you?"

"I didn't." If I'd thought of it, I would have. "But it must be a sign for us to tell Benjie about this."

A look of horror crossed her features. "Not like this," she hissed. "He can't find me in your bed. That's a terrible way to find out." She whimpered when we both heard the pitter-patter of footsteps.

Brooke dropped to the floor to hide. It was the side of the bed away from the door, so Benjie wouldn't see her at least. Even when I just wanted to come clean with Benjie, I wouldn't do it unless Brooke was on board.

Grabbing the blanket, I sat to lean against the headboard and pulled it up over my waist in time for Benjie to open my door.

"Morning, buddy."

"Morning." He smiled. He seemed chirpier than usual. "Can we have pancakes for breakfast?"

"We sure can. Why don't you go get the things ready while I have a quick shower?"

"Okay." His smile grew as he rocked on his feet a little. What he didn't do was leave.

"Was there something else you needed, kiddo?"

"Well, I just wanted to know if Miss Brooke can come have breakfast?"

"Ah, I'm sure she'd like that. I'll call her shortly, all right?"

"Why?"

"Why what, Benjie?"

"Why call her when she's lying on the floor?"

Something banged. I had a feeling it was Brooke's head from her quiet curse.

"Benjie—"

"Is she your girlfriend now?"

"Ah…." Did I tell him now or would Brooke kill me? I didn't want to die after confessing my love for her and her for me.

A sigh sounded from the side of the bed before Brooke stood and gave a wave to Benjie, her face turning bright red. "Hi, Benjie. I just stopped by this morning to check on Dustin because…." She looked to me for help, but my brain was out of action.

"Huh? But I went to the bathroom really early and saw you and Daddy sleeping in bed, but your phone started making a noise and I didn't want it to wake you both. I quickly snuck in to turn it off. I didn't do anything wrong, did I?"

Brooke's gaze softened. "No, buddy, you didn't, and I, um, did stay the night. I hope that was okay."

His smile was back as he rolled his eyes. "You're Daddy's girlfriend now, right? Daddy said only special people stay over, like wives and girlfriends. It must mean you're his girlfriend so it's okay."

"It does mean I'm his girlfriend, as long as you're okay with it."

His tiny fists shook around in the air, and he yelled, "Yay, I've been wanting this for ages, because it means you can come around all the time when I'm here now and we can do so much."

Brooke's eyes filled with tears and she nodded. "I'll look forward to it, but for now, how about we get those pancakes ready?"

Benjie nodded enthusiastically.

Brooke started to move around the bed, but I said, "Benjie, I need to have a word with Brooke. We'll meet you in the kitchen."

His nose screwed up. "Is this where you guys are going to kiss?"

Chuckling, I shrugged. "It might be."

"Okay" was all he said before he skipped out of the room.

Scooting over to a frozen Brooke, I climbed out of bed and pulled her into my arms. Her breath escaped her in a huff when she wrapped her arms around my waist and buried her face in my chest.

"What was it you said about Benjie finding out you stayed the night?"

A fist landed in my side.

Chuckling, I pulled back and cupped both sides of her neck. "He loves you, darlin', so there's nothing to worry about. He's like his daddy when it comes to opening our hearts to certain people. It doesn't happen often, but when it does, that person is stuck with us."

She sniffed. "He's just too adorable."

"Even when those tantrums come out?" He'd had a few now when Brooke was around, not that any fazed her. She eventually talked him down with her magical powers.

"Even then. And when yours come out."

"Aww, I was even adorable when I cried about not being able to give you head the other night?"

She snorted. "Well, except then. Your man card lowered a few notches and I thought about breaking up with you." She lifted her gaze. "But then I realized I was in love with you. Gross, right?"

Grinning like a lovesick fool, I scrunched my nose up. "Ew, that is gross, especially when it's catching, and I love you back."

"How long do you think we have before he comes to look for us?" she asked as her hand slipped into my briefs and gripped my hardening dick.

"I don't think we have that long."

She pouted. "Too bad." She pulled her hand free, patted my chest, and moved around me toward the door.

"Later?" I whimpered.

"Later." She winked over her shoulder.

Goddamn, I was in love with her. Forgoing the shower until after breakfast, where I hoped I could talk Brooke into having one with me while I set Benjie up with his new LEGO set, I dressed in tracksuit pants and a tee before I followed after my woman.

"Benjie, give me the phone," I heard as I rounded the corner to see Benjie cackling as he ran around the middle island with Brooke chasing him.

"Yes, Mr. Tom. She stayed here last night and said she was his girlfriend."

My eyes widened.

"You want to come to dinner later? Last night Daddy said that Mr. North and his mister is coming over with Miss Reagan and Mr. Carter." He slipped out of Brooke's reach. "Okay. Six. Yes, bye." He hung up and handed the phone to Brooke.

"Benjie, were you on Brooke's phone?"

"Nope. It was the home phone."

"Benjie, why were you talking to Tom?"

"I called him after Nana Bev." He'd met her on a few occasions when we went there for Friday dinner night.

"Wait, what?" Brooke screeched.

"Why did you call Tom, Benjie?"

"He wanted me to tell him when you two started dating. He said he needs to have an important word with you, Daddy."

Did I run for the hills now?

Only when I looked at Brooke, who seemed either angry or scared or a bit of both, I knew I'd take on the world for her.

"Oh, and they're all coming for dinner." He skipped up to Brooke and hugged her legs. Looking up to her, he asked, "Can I just call you Brooke? You're like family now so it's okay to, right?"

Brooke melted under his words, and I knew the worry about dinner with everyone was brushed aside by Benjie's words. She gently pushed his hair away from his eyes. "I would be very happy if you did."

"Okay... Brooke."

Dipping, she kissed his cheek. "Thank you for being so cool, buddy."

Benjie shrugged. "You're welcome. Can we get breakfast now? I'm hungry."

"Of course we can."

Brooke moved over to the oven, but I slipped up behind her and wrapped my arms around her middle. "How you doing?"

She sniffed. "Fine."

Chuckling, I kissed her shoulder. "Liar."

"I just... I'm happy."

"I'm glad you are, darlin', because both Benjie and I are as well. Especially when you're around."

She turned in my arms and rested her hands on my waist. "Thank you for being a pain and pestering me about dating."

I grinned. "Thank you for finally giving in and accepting. We'll also have to thank Nana Bev again. If it wasn't for her, I doubt I would have been so lucky."

She nodded. "This is true. I'll cook—" My eyes widened, and she sighed. "I'll have you cook her favorite baked potatoes with all the trimmings and creamy mustard chicken."

"I can do that." Brooke still wasn't the best cook, even after I'd tried teaching her. It was like everything she touched was repelled by her lack of skills or just didn't want to end up charcoaled. Not that I cared if she cooked or not. I didn't mind cooking. I'd always been a fan of it, finding it relaxing. If I wasn't up for cooking, there were plenty of takeout options.

"I will master it one day. I'll make cooking my bitch."

Patting her head, which she swatted away, I kissed her nose. "I'm sure you will." Glancing around to my son, I added, "Don't you think Benjie... Benjie?"

"Where did he go?"

A tiny, what was trying to be quiet voice, was heard from the living room. "I know, Mommy, it's the best. Brooke will be around all the time now."

Brooke's wide gaze shot up to mine.

Chuckling, I shrugged. "He's happy about us being together."

"He's a little gossiper like his father."

"Who, me?"

"Yes, you. You told Carter about—"

"Do you think Brooke will love me like she does Daddy, because she'd have to love him if she wants to be his girl-friend? But can she love me too?"

Brooke's bottom lip quivered before she bolted into the living room and swung Benjie up into her arms and mumbled into his neck.

"What?" Benjie asked.

My damn chest felt heavy from all the blissful emotions swimming inside it. "She said she loves you with her whole heart."

Benjie wrapped his arms around her neck. "I love you too!"

Taking the phone from Benjie, I lifted it to my ear. "Em?" All I could hear on the other end was my ex crying. Brooke and Emily had grown close, to the point where Emily ended up going to girls' night with Brooke, Reagan, and Courtney.

"It's so sweet," she yelled through the phone before bursting into fresh tears.

Never would I take for granted how lucky I was to have these people in my life, but I'd thank anyone or everyone I could who made it possible. Without a damn doubt, I was blessed.

CHAPTER NINETEEN

BROOKE

*W*e didn't exactly have enough room for everyone for dinner since Tom opened his mouth to Reagan's parents, and they arrived with him, so we had to bring in an extra table and chair from Dustin's garage. Though, currently Tom didn't look too happy about Herb and Elaine arriving when he did.

"This was my time with them. Alone. I shouldn't have said anything to you on the phone," Tom complained as he entered the living room with them in tow.

Herb scoffed. "I'd thought we'd come to the agreement to share?"

Tom glared. "Only because I was getting more time with them."

"Who is them, exactly?" Reagan asked from the couch

were she and I sat. We already knew they were talking about the men, but it was fun to get a reaction out of them and their fanboying over the guys. I doubted Herb and Tom would ever get over the fact they had a close connection to some of the men on the Wolves team. Every time they acted like teenagers seeing a singer they adored for the first time.

"Hey, Elaine, look at this over here." Herb moved across the living room to stare out the window. He pretended to point something out to his wife, who rolled her eyes, patted his back, and moved off into the kitchen.

"Tom, I thought you were here to talk to Dustin about something? That's what Benjie said."

Dustin, who was talking to Carter off to the side, glowered at me.

Tom rubbed at the back of his neck. "Yes, well, I think since he's welcomed me into his house, I'll leave the talk for another day. Then again, I'm sure he took our warning at dinner that night seriously."

Dustin nodded. "I did."

"Good." Tom crossed his arms over his chest.

Herb made a noise in the back of his throat. It kind of sounded like a whimper. When he turned, his cheeks seemed red. He cleared his throat and made his way toward the hall.

"Dad, where are you going?" Reagan asked.

"Nowhere." His strides increased.

Carter chuckled. "I'm guessing North and Jennings are here."

Tom gasped. He raced for the hallway. We heard a crash and then cursing with a few heated words.

"Dustin, do you want to go save your teammates?" I asked.

He placed his hand to his ear. "I think I hear Benjie calling me." His smirk said it all. He was going to leave North and Jennings to suffer on their own.

"Dustin, don't you dare." He'd already bolted for the bedrooms where Benjie was playing.

Reagan sighed. "Carter…."

"Coming, Benjie," Carter called and walked off.

"Come on, it's up to us." I stood with Reagan, and we quickly made it down the hall to the front door where we saw Tom and Herb peeking out the frosted glass panels on each side of it.

"Guys, come on. Let them arrive in peace." So they didn't get too scared over their fawning.

"But—" A knock sounded, and their eyes widened before they looked at each other and snickered like little kids.

"Dad, Tom, living room, now, or you'll never be invited over again," Reagan threatened. They glowered at her and shuffled down the hall sulking. "I'll watch them. You answer the door."

"Good idea." As soon as I saw Reagan walking down the hall and into the living room, I opened the front door with a smile. "Hey, guys. Thanks for coming."

"Thanks for the invite." North smiled as he stepped in and kissed my cheek. If I wasn't with Dustin, I would have swooned, but Dustin had ruined my attraction for anyone else.

North moved to the side and Jennings stepped in but halted at my words. "Ah, there's a few extra people here. Reagan's parents and our boss from school. Benjie's fault." Yes, I threw the kid under the bus. "He invited Tom this morning and the others followed him. On the bright side, it's pure luck my nana was busy and couldn't make it. She'd probably question you about who topped and bottomed."

Jennings spun around and started for the car. North laughed and quickly grabbed him before he could get far. "It'll be fine," he told Jennings, who grumbled something.

When North had Jennings inside, I quickly closed the front door. "Another word of warning." I winced at Jennings's hard stare and clenched jaw. "Tom and Herb are massive fans, but they're also family. Nothing will leave the house that you don't want. They're very trustworthy."

Jennings cursed a few times. "You know I don't do well around people." He glared at his lover.

North kissed his cheek and took his hand. "You'll be fine."

"I swear to God, if you leave my fucking side, I'll kick your ass."

North chuckled. "I won't."

The nerves were coming off Jennings in waves as he stepped into the living room. Since I knew Tom and Herb, I also knew it wouldn't take them long to have Jennings relaxed.

Reagan cursed when they slipped out of her hold and stepped in front of North and Jennings.

Dear God, they bowed their heads slightly and looked at them in awe. Did Tom have a few tears in his eyes?

Tom opened his mouth, but before he said anything, Herb did. "Hi, welcome, it's great to meet you both. I—"

"Your dick's hanging out," Tom suddenly said, causing Herb to blush and actually look down at his crotch.

North choked on a laugh, and even Jennings's lips twitched.

"Dad, why in the heck would you look down?"

Tom smirked. "Because it happened—"

"One time! Just once when I was too drunk and forgot to put it away after I went to the bathroom."

Reagan groaned and slapped her forehead. "I could have gone without knowing that."

Laughing, I shook my head.

"Hi, I'm Tom. I work with Reagan and Brooke. It's an honor to meet you both, North and Jack." He held his hand out, and North went to take it, until Herb slapped it away and took it instead. "Dickhead," Tom muttered and quickly grabbed Jennings's hand and shook it.

"You know, my daughter is with Carter, but I have a niece—"

Tom slapped Herb in the back of the head and gestured to North's and Jennings's joined hands. Jennings tried to pull his hand free, but North wouldn't have it.

"Ah." Herb nodded. "Well, I don't have any sons or nephews, but Carter has brothers. I'm sure— Will you quit hitting me." Herb scowled at Tom.

"It was me this time." Elaine popped up out of nowhere. "Hi, I'm Elaine. Reagan's mother, and I suppose I can claim to being this dense head's wife. It's nice to meet you both. Can you tell me which one of you bottoms and—" Reagan ran forward and covered her mother's mouth.

Snorting out a laugh, I shrugged at North and Jennings's shocked looks. "Guess I didn't need my nana here for that question. Guys, how about we let North and Jennings move into the house more and give them some breathing room."

Tom nodded a little too much as he shifted back. "Of course. Can I get either of you a drink? Dinner's about ready, I'm sure, but if you need a snack, I can get you one."

"I'm fine, thanks, Tom," North said.

Tom straightened, and his eyes glistened a little.

"I can help also," Herb added.

"Where's Carter and Dustin?" North asked.

"They're hiding in Benjie's room so you two could get the full welcome party from Tom and Herb on your own."

"What do you mean?" Tom asked.

"Yeah, we've been nice." Herb crossed his arms over his chest.

"Nothing." I smiled.

"Can I kill your friends?" Jennings muttered as Elaine pulled Herb and Tom away.

North nodded. "I'll even help."

A little monster barreled into my side and hugged my waist. "Hi, Mr. North and Mr...." Benjie looked up to me. "Do I call him scary man like Daddy does? Or should I say Jack or Jennings?"

"Hey, hey, hey, kiddo. I never said Jack was a scary man." Dustin chuckled guiltily and rested his hands on Benjie's shoulders as Carter snorted and shook the guys' hands. "I said he was my new best friend."

"You said that eventually, Daddy. But I heard you on the phone to Mr. Carter—" Dustin covered his son's mouth while I snorted and thought we really had to make sure Benjie wasn't around when we were trying to have a private conversation.

Jennings's brows drew up as he stared at Dustin.

"Anyway. Dinner's ready." Dustin bolted back into the kitchen, taking Benjie with him.

"Are you sure he's your friend?" Jennings asked North.

North snorted. "Yeah, he grows on you."

That he did, and in the best ways. Before Jennings knew it, Dustin would have wormed his way into becoming close friends.

LEANING BACK IN MY SEAT, I LISTENED TO THE CONVERSATIONS around me and smiled. It was good to see everyone relaxed and talking. Even Jennings tried to involve himself. I knew it was more for North's sake because every time he spoke or started a conversation, he would look to North to see if he was noticing. North definitely was; his eyes didn't move far from Jennings at all.

Dustin's arm curled around my shoulders, and he gently tugged me into his side before he kissed my temple. "Having fun?"

Grinning up at him, I kissed his chin. "Yes. It's good to see everyone together. We're only missing Nana and the Diamond MC guys."

He chuckled. "We'd need a bigger house if that was to happen."

We'd.

He'd said *we* would need a bigger house.

My heart and stomach were singing and dancing together. I knew Dustin and I were working toward a future, but it was good to hear us moving in together come out of Dustin's mouth.

Snuggling back into him, I nipped at his hand over my shoulder. "Can you imagine a dinner party with Adrik, Death, and State?"

Dustin grinned. "There'd be a few more death threats going around if anyone looked at their partners wrong."

"And if Nana was there, a lot of them would be said to her."

We both laughed, and from across the table, I caught Benjie staring at us with a smile. I was so glad he was happy with our relationship.

Dustin cleared his throat and then announced to the table, "Just in case no one knew by now, Brooke and I are dating." I knew he'd said it for Benjie's sake since he only found out today.

Elaine gasped and pressed her hands to her chest. Everyone looked at her. "What? Too much?"

"Just a little." Herb patted her on the head. "It was plain to see after we arrived, and you haven't left Brooke's side for a second."

"I think it's awesome." Benjie clapped.

"Thank you, buddy." I smiled softly as my chest warmed.

"It means I could get a brother or a sister soon. If I get a choice, I want a brother so we can play LEGO together."

Dustin choked on his sip of beer, and I quickly shook my head. "Buddy, it's too soon for that. Besides, I still have Val to take care of since she's only a little baby."

"I suppose." He shrugged. "At least you didn't say it wouldn't happen."

He had me there.

Dustin's hand slid under my hair and cupped the back of my neck. As the others went to talk about something else, I looked up to Dustin when he shook me slightly. He smiled. "At least you didn't say it wouldn't happen."

I knew he'd said it before, but I had the urge to check again. "You want more children?"

"Darlin', eventually I want it all with you." He pressed his lips to mine, but I was still stunned by his words.

He wanted it all with me.

That meant living together, marriage, and kids... right?

It did.

Gripping his thigh, I leaned in and told him, "You're getting an extra-long blow job for that."

"Damn, darlin', you're making me hard at the dinner table."

"It's your fault for being... well, you."

He pulled back and winked. "You know, with that offer, it tells me that you really do love me."

Nodding, I solemnly said, "You've ruined me for anyone else."

Dustin chuckled and lightly pecked my lips. "Good, because you've done the same."

EPILOGUE

BROOKE

*T*here, over there. Do you see him, Brooke?" Benjie yelled from right beside me as he clutched my hand in one of his. The other he used to point out his father on the field. He'd grown up so much in the past year, and I wondered if putting a brick on his head would slow it down.

"I sure do." And damn, Dustin looked mighty fine. My belly gave that excited twisted thrill when I thought about the fact that I'd moved in with him about three months ago. He'd asked me when we'd been over at Nana Bev's for dinner. Maybe he'd been worried I'd say no and wanted backup from Nana, but he hadn't needed it.

I took one look at him and Benjie and knew my answer.

I loved going to sleep and waking up with him. Even if he did hog all the blankets. Then there were the mornings and nights when Benjie was here. The more time with them, the more I thought of them as my own little family, and I couldn't help but smile goofily over how lucky I was, my body warming, knowing they were my people.

Not to say life was always picture perfect.

Dustin still annoyed me or pissed me off, and I did the same with him. I would take all and any day, happy or bad, though, and bottle them in my memory box, as I couldn't imagine my life without Dustin and Benjie in it.

Val was also content in her new place.

Of course, as soon as Benjie was home, she deserted me and slept on his bed. I wasn't jealous at all. All right, I was a little. She'd been my girl for so long. At least I had someone else to cuddle with, and Dustin was very good at snuggling.

"Never been to a game in person before." Nana Bev stepped up beside me with the help of Tom. "This is pretty exciting. So much eye candy to look at."

"What's eye candy?" Benjie asked.

Shooting a glare at Nana, who cackled, I told Benjie, "She's talking about the candy at the concession stand."

Tom snorted.

"Oh." Benjie's lips thinned. "I'd like some eye candy."

Groaning under my breath, I sent Nana another death glare.

She grinned. "Don't worry, dear boy, you'll get some when you're older."

"Nana—"

"How about I take Benjie to the concession stand?"

"But there's a person who comes to the family box," Benjie said.

"That's okay, I could use a walk. Will you keep me company?" Tom held his hand out, and Benjie nodded with a smile before he took it.

Once they were gone, I glanced around at the people in the box. I didn't know everyone was coming to the game when I said I'd meet Emily and her man here to do the switch over since Benjie would be with her tonight. I also didn't expect her to stay for the game, but I was glad she did. She stood chatting with Courtney and Reagan, while her man spoke with State, Carter, and Herb. Even Elaine was here and she wasn't a fan of football like her husband, Herb.

"It's good to see you happy, boo."

Glancing back to Nana, I smiled warmly. "It's good to feel happy."

"You sure no woman will tempt you away from that man of yours?"

Rolling my eyes, I leaned my hip into the wall separating us from the field to face Nana. "Did Dustin put you up to that question?"

She snorted. "No... yes."

"He has nothing to worry about. I'm completely in love with him."

Nana's gaze softened before it sparked with mischief. "He must be good in bed then."

"Nana, I love you, but I'm not giving you any details about Dustin in bed."

"Dang it. You're supposed to let me live vicariously through you."

"Please, you're dating card is and always has been bigger

than mine. I know you're not going without... and I could have done without thinking that."

She cackled before sobering. "Still, I just want you to know your parents would be so proud and happy with how you've led your life. Just like I am."

The words hit me right in the chest.

"Thanks, Nana," I whispered.

"I could still go for a great-grandbaby, so get on that, yeah?"

Laughing, I shook my head. "I'll see what I can do. You could pester Reagan more. At least she's married already. You never know, she might be knocked up now."

"Reagan," she yelled across the family box. "Are you knocked up yet?"

Reagan paled and shot her gaze to Carter.

Wait.

Holy shit, she was?

I slapped a hand over my mouth, my eyes widening.

"Wait, are you?" Elaine asked.

Carter sighed. "We only found out today."

"Oh. My. God!" Elaine screamed as she jumped up and down.

"Mom, you can't tell anyone else. Well, besides the rest of Carter's family. But I'm only seven weeks along."

Elaine burst into tears. Even Herb was misty-eyed as he pulled Carter into a hug. I made my way over to Reagan and dragged her into a hug before her mom got to her.

"I'm so goddamn happy for you, but sorry about Nana. I was getting her off my back."

She laughed. "It's fine."

Pulling back, I grabbed her shoulders and shook her a little. Tears formed in my eyes. "You're pregnant."

"I am."

"You're going to have to squeeze a watermelon out of your vagina."

She sniffed. "I know."

"Love you, girlfriend."

"Love you more, and I'm so darn happy you're happy, and I'm happy and—"

"We're all happy."

She snorted out another laugh as I shook her shoulders again. "Yes." She nodded.

Elaine, Herb, and somehow Tom had appeared again, all surrounding her for a group hug, which I just escaped. I was sure I even heard Tom blubbering about how amazing it was she was going to have an ex-Wolves player's baby.

Courtney had her arm wrapped around her brother, crying into his arm. "We have to call Mom and Dad now!"

"Court, we're going to see them after the game."

"Dominic, we're going with them. I want to see their faces. Oh, oh, call the brothers and have them meet us there."

Smiling, I moved over to Benjie, Emily, her man, and Nana, who winced. "Did I fuck up?" she muttered when I got to her side.

"No, it would have come out soon anyway."

"What's everyone crying about?" Benjie asked.

Emily glanced at me quickly; we all knew Benjie was a gossip. Emily ruffled his hair as he leaned back into her legs. "They're all just happy to be here and watching the team play. Did you see your daddy score that last touchdown?"

"I sure did. He was awesome."

With the news, I felt a little guilty, as I hadn't been paying much attention to the game. Though, as soon as Dustin found out Reagan was pregnant, I was sure he'd forgive me.

"Come on, how about we snack while we watch the rest of the game? Nana, let's get you a seat."

After a while, everyone settled into their seats again to finish watching the close game. I knew Dustin would play to all his strengths, since I'd promised him a blow job on the drive home. Actually, I was looking forward to a night with just the two of us. We could be as loud as we wanted without worrying Benjie would overhear. I also had a cute new lingerie set I wanted to share with my man.

In the last few minutes of the game, we were all on the edge of our seats. It was a tie, and the Wolves had the ball. Jennings threw it to North, who dodged around someone grabbing for him and passed it to Dustin. We all screamed and cheered him on, until I held my breath when I saw someone coming close to him. Dustin slid to the side and tossed the ball to Jennings, who took it right into the end zone to win the game.

Hugs went all around, and a few tears followed—mainly from Herb and Tom. Benjie leaped onto my lap and wrapped his arms around my neck.

"They won!"

"They did." I grinned.

Suddenly there was a screech over the loudspeaker, before a voice came over, "Ladies and gentlemen, we just have one last announcement. Just bear with us for a moment as the Wolves get into position."

Benjie slid off my lap and moved over to Emily.

"What's going on?" Herb asked.

"Don't tell me someone's leaving the team again," Tom whined.

Looking out onto the field, I saw Dustin's team jogging over toward our family box. Standing, I gripped my top. "Is Dustin okay?" I asked, only no one said anything. I caught North and Jennings at the front in the middle as they stopped right in front of us. North winked, and even Jennings had a small smile, which was big for him.

My heart jumped into my throat when Dustin's voice sounded from behind them.

"I know you hated me when I stuffed things up after we'd first met, and I understood why you were hesitant to want a relationship with me." Tears filled my eyes. I glanced at Benjie and his smile was radiant when he gave me two thumbs up.

Dustin's team parted and there stood my sweaty, dirty man as he went on, saying, "But the day you gave me a chance and admitted how awesome I was that you couldn't resist dating me any longer." I snorted out a laugh and wiped at my eyes. "It changed my life for the better. If you give me one more chance, I promise to make our future the best it can be." Dustin stepped through his teammates and walked my way. People cheered but stopped quickly when Dustin jumped the wall separating us and got to one knee. "Brooke Baker, will you do me the honor of becoming my wife?"

Elation bubbled up inside me, causing me to blurt, "You're an asshole for making me cry."

Dustin chuckled. "Is that a yes? Can I always be *your* asshole?"

"Yes. Yes!" I nodded. More tears filled my eyes and tumbled over, just like my stomach was doing. While my heart, there wasn't anything I could do to stop the frantic beat of nerves, excitement, and love.

Dustin slid the ring on my finger before he stood and scooped me up into his arms. I wrapped mine around his neck, ignoring his pads, and held him tightly.

"Love you, darlin'." He pressed a kiss to my cheek.

Pulling back, I cupped his face. "I'll always love you, even when you piss me off." He chuckled, but it tapered off when I leaned in and kissed him.

More cheers and whistles filled the air. Then small arms curled around our sides as Dustin placed me back on my feet. I couldn't quit smiling, and Dustin was having the same problem.

Dustin bent and picked Benjie up, who dragged us into a three-way hug. I didn't put up a fight though. These people were my future, and I couldn't wait to see where it would go.

ALSO BY LILA ROSE

Hawks MC: Ballarat Charter

Holding Out (Free)

Outplayed (standalone related to the Hawks MC)

Climbing Out

Finding Out (novella)

Black Out

No Way Out

Coming Out (m/m novella)

Out to Find Freedom (standalone related to the Hawks MC)

Hawks MC: Caroline Springs Charter

The Secret's Out

Hiding Out

Down and Out

Living Without

Walkout (novella)

Hear Me Out (m/m)

Break Out (novella)

Fallout

Out of the Blue (standalone related to the Hawks MC: m/m/m)

Out Gamed (standalone related to the Hawks MC: novella)

Hawks MC: next generation

Coyote

Ruin (m/m)

Romantic Comedies

Making Changes

Making Sense

Fumbled Love

Bumbled Love

Polished P & P series (m/m romance)

Wreck Me Forever

Never a Saint

Working Out West

Trinity Love Series

Left to Chance (m/m/f novel)

Love of Liberty (m/m/f novella)

Standalones

In The Dark (paranormal)

Havoc's Mate (paranormal novella)

Senseless Attraction (Y/A)

TITLES UNDER L. ROSE

The Hidden Kingdom Trilogy

(reverse harem romance)

A Torn Paige

A Lost Paige

A Final Paige

CONNECT WITH LILA ROSE

Webpage: www.lilarosebooks.com

Facebook: http://bit.ly/2du0taO

Instagram: www.instagram.com/lilarose78/

Goodreads:

www.goodreads.com/author/show/7236200.Lila_Rose